It Was Fascinating, *Shattering,* This Glimpse Into His Past.

Another reminder that she hadn't known him at all, another proof of how unimportant she'd been— that he hadn't shared this with her, clearly a major incident in his life.

But it was worse than that. She'd believed he'd been born without the capacity for emotional involvement. It had been what had mitigated her heartache and humiliation. Believing he'd never given her what he hadn't had to give.

But his emotions existed. And they could be powerful, pure. It seemed that it took something profound to unearth it, like what he'd shared with others. Not as trivial as what he had with her.

The discovery had the knife that had long stopped turning in her heart stabbing it all over again.

Dear Reader,

Writing Haidar Aal Shalaan's story was a surprise with each word. He first appeared in Pride of Zohayd, his half brothers' trilogy. In the last book, *To Touch a Sheikh,* he found out his mother was conspiring to depose his father and brothers to make him king. But even though he did all he could to abort her conspiracy, I knew then that it wouldn't end with him a hero and the near-catastrophe forgotten, or forgiven.

And it wasn't, least of all by him. As I wrote his story, he showed me his turmoil over his dichotomy, a man both blessed and cursed by birth. He shared with me how he'd had to fight all his life against what he thought to be his inherited nature, which he believed had cost him everyone he'd ever loved and stigmatized him forever. He was on a mission to redeem himself from the taint of his mother's treachery, and to reclaim his heart from the woman who'd once trodden all over it. I thought he'd be a stoic, vengeful, hot-blooded knight of the desert as he accomplished both missions.

But he kept surprising me, demonstrating his duality in every word and action. He was fierce yet tender, unyielding yet flexible, unstoppable yet vulnerable and most of all, the last thing I expected him to be, he was funny. And fun. And boy, was he irresistible for it. His heroine, Roxanne, wholeheartedly agrees.

I truly hope you enjoy Haidar and his journey toward making peace with himself—and finally loving Roxanne well—as much as I did.

I love to hear from readers, so email me at oliviagates@gmail.com. And please stay connected with me on Facebook at my fan page, Olivia Gates Author, and on Twitter, @OliviaGates.

Thanks for reading!

Olivia

OLIVIA GATES

THE SHEIKH'S REDEMPTION

Harlequin®

Desire

Recycling programs
for this product may
not exist in your area.

ISBN-13: 978-0-373-73178-7

THE SHEIKH'S REDEMPTION

www.Harlequin.com

Printed in U.S.A.

Books by Olivia Gates

Harlequin Desire

The Sarantos Secret Baby #2080
**To Touch a Sheikh* #2103
A Secret Birthright #2136
††*The Sheikh's Redemption* #2165

Silhouette Desire

The Desert Lord's Baby #1872
The Desert Lord's Bride #1884
The Desert King #1896
†*The Once and Future Prince* #1942
†*The Prodigal Prince's Seduction* #1948
†*The Illegitimate King* #1954
Billionaire, M.D. #2005
In Too Deep #2025
   "The Sheikh's Bargained Bride"
**To Tame a Sheikh* #2050
**To Tempt a Sheikh* #2069

*Throne of Judar
†The Castaldini Crown
**Pride of Zohayd
††Desert Knights

Other titles by this author available in ebook format.

OLIVIA GATES

has always pursued creative passions such as singing and handicrafts. She still does, but only one of her passions grew gratifying enough, consuming enough, to become an ongoing career—writing.

She is most fulfilled when she is creating worlds and conflicts for her characters, then exploring and untangling them bit by bit, sharing her protagonists' every heart-wrenching heartache and hope, their every heart-pounding doubt and trial, until she leads them to an indisputably earned and gloriously satisfying happy ending.

When she's not writing, she is a doctor, a wife to her own alpha male and a mother to one brilliant girl and one demanding Angora cat. Visit Olivia at www.oliviagates.com.

To my mom. The most courageous, persevering and accomplished woman I know. Thanks for being you.

Prologue

Twenty-four years ago

The slap fell on Haidar's face, stinging it on fire.

Before he could gasp, another fell on his other cheek, harder, backhanded this time. A ring encrusted in precious stones dragged a ragged line of pain into his flesh.

Disoriented, he heard a crack of thunder as tears misted his sight. Admonishments boomed again as more slaps tossed Haidar's head from side to side. One finally shattered his balance, sent him crashing to his knees. Tears singed the fresh cut like a harsh antiseptic, mingling with the blood.

A tranquil voice broke over him. "Shed more tears, Haidar, and I'll have you thrown in the dungeon. For a week."

He swallowed, stared up at the person he loved most in life, incomprehension paralyzing him.

Why was she *doing* this?

His mother had never laid a hand on him. He'd never even gotten the knuckle raps or ear twists his twin, Jalal, drove her to reward his mischief with. He was her favorite. She told him so, showed him her esteem and preference in every way.

But there *had* been times lately when she'd been displeased with him, when he'd done nothing wrong. Actually, when he'd done something praiseworthy. It had bewildered him. Still, nothing could have prepared him for her out-of-the-blue, ice-cold fury just when he'd expected her to shower him with approval.

She stared down from her majestic height, looking as he'd always imagined a goddess of myth would, her eyes arctic. "Don't compound your stupidity with whimpering. Stand up and take your punishment like your twin always does—with dignity and courage."

Haidar almost blurted out that it was Jalal—*and* their cousin Rashid—who deserved the punishment. The "experiment" he'd warned them against and had refused to take part in had caused the fire that had consumed a whole chamber in the palace and ruined his and Jalal's tenth birthday party.

Being habitually wild and reckless, Jalal and Rashid had long depleted their second chances with their elders. Their punishment would have been severe. Being the one with a track record of caution and commitment, his reserve of leniency was intact. So he'd stepped forward as the accidental culprit.

Just when his confession had garnered what he'd expected from his and Jalal's father and Rashid's guardian—surprise followed by acceptance of his explanation and dismissal of the whole debacle—his mother had walked up to him.

Her eyes had told him she knew what had really happened, and why he'd stepped forward. He'd expected admiration to follow the shrewdness that made him feel she could read his slightest thought. What had followed were the slaps that hadn't stopped even when her husband, the king of Zohayd, had ordered her to cease.

Haidar rose and lifted a trembling hand to the sticky warmth oozing across his left cheekbone. She swatted it away.

"Now beg your twin's and cousin's forgiveness for being slow in coming clean about your thoughtless transgression, almost causing them to be punished in your stead."

Disbelief numbed him, chagrin seared his chest. It was one thing to take punishment for them, another to apologize *to* them, and in front of everyone present, relatives, servants… *girls!*

His mother clamped his face in a vicious grip, her long nails digging into his wound. *"Do it."*

She released him with a shove, made him stumble around to face Jalal and Rashid. They were staring at their feet, faces red, chests heaving.

"Jalal, Rashid, look at Haidar." His mother now spoke as Queen Sondoss of Zohayd, her voice clear and commanding, carrying to the whole ballroom. "Don't spare him the disgrace of groveling for your forgiveness in front of everyone."

Jalal's and Rashid's gazes wavered up to her before turning to him, apology and contrition blazing in their eyes.

His mother prodded him with a head whack. "Tell them you're sorry, that you'll *never* do anything like this again."

Burning with mortification, he looked into his twin's eyes, then into his distant cousin and best friend's, and repeated her words.

"I didn't do it!"

Haidar blurted the words out as his mother finished dressing his wound. Now that they were in the privacy of her chambers, he had to exonerate himself, if only in her eyes.

Her smile was filled with pride and love as she kissed the injury she'd inflicted. "I know." So he'd been right! "I know everything. Certainly about you and Jalal and that rascal Rashid."

His confusion deepened. "Then…*why?*"

She cupped his cheek tenderly. "It was a lesson, Haidar.

I wanted to show you that even your twin and best friend wouldn't say a word to spare you. Now you know that no one deserves your intervention or sacrifice. Now you know to trust no one. Most important, you know what humiliation feels like, and you'll always do anything you must to never suffer it again."

His head spun at her explanations, their implications.

He didn't want to believe her, but—she was always right.

Was she about this, too?

She came down beside him, hugged him. "You're the only true part of me and I'll do anything so that you never get hurt, so that you become the man who will get everything you deserve. This world at your feet. Do you understand why I had to hurt you?"

Shaken by the new perspective she'd shown him, he nodded. Mainly because he wanted to get away, to think.

She stroked his hair and crooned, "That's my boy."

Eight years ago

"You're just like Mother."

Haidar flinched as if from a teeth-loosening slap.

Jalal was twisting the knife that had been embedded in his chest ever since they'd been old enough to realize what their mother was. What she was called. The Demon Queen.

To Haidar's heartache, no matter his personal feelings for her, he'd been forced to concede the title had been well earned.

While his mother possessed unearthly beauty and breathtaking intelligence and talents, she wielded her endowments like lethal weapons. She flaunted being *unpolluted* by the foolish weakness of benevolence. Instead of using her blessings to gain allies, she collected cowed servants and cohorts. And she relished making enemies, the first of which being her own husband.

If it weren't for her fierce love for her sons, or for him mainly and to a lesser degree, for Jalal, he would have doubted she was human at all.

But what had always tormented Haidar was that the older he got, the more he realized what a "true part" of her he was. He'd felt the taint of her temperament, the chronic disease of her traits spreading inside him. He'd lived in fear that they'd one day obliterate his decent and compassionate components.

It was ironic that Jalal had thrown that similarity in his face now, when he'd been feeling his mother's shadow recede, her legacy loosening its noose from around his thoughts and inclinations. Ever since he'd met Roxanne...

"I take it back." Jalal, the twin who resembled him the least of probably anyone in the world, shook his head in disgust. "You're worse than her. And *that* I didn't think was possible."

"You talk as if she's a monster."

They'd never spoken this openly about their mother. They'd been speaking less and less about anything at all.

Jalal shrugged, the movement nonchalant but eloquent with leashed force. A reminder that though they were similar in size and strength, Jalal was the...physical one.

"And I love her nonetheless. But that's the unreasoning affection a mother wrings from her child. You don't get the same leniency. Not on *this*. This is one instance where I cannot, *will* not, rationalize or forgive your heartlessness."

Unable to deal with his twin's disapproval any better than he ever had, he let the fury and suspicion that had brought him to this confrontation take over. "So this is your strategy? Like they say in Azmahar, 'Yell accusations lest your opponent beats you'?"

"It's you who are resorting to 'Hit and weep, preempt and cry foul.'"

Jalal's derision scraped his already raw nerves. "I never suspected you'd be such a sore loser when Roxanne chose me."

Jalal snorted, his eyes smoldering like black ice. "You mean when she was manipulated by you. *Conned* by you."

Haidar suppressed another spurt of indignation, the frost at his core resurfacing. "Can't find a more realistic excuse for trying to steal her from me? We both know I can get any woman I want without even trying, no manipulation involved."

"You couldn't have gotten Roxanne without it. She saw you for the ice-cold fish that you are that first night. It must have taken some Academy Award–winning acting to create the fictional character that she fell for."

Haidar had never resorted to violence, not even while growing up among an abundance of male-only relatives who relished rough…resolutions. He'd always suppressed his temper, used cold deliberation to outmaneuver them. Now he wanted to smash in Jalal's well-arranged face.

He gritted down on the urge. "The fact remains—she's *mine*."

"And you have been treating her like property. Worse, like a dirty secret, making her hide your intimacies from even her mother, forcing her to watch you flaunt the other women 'you have without even trying' in public. You told her they're decoys to draw suspicion away from her, right? It must be killing her, even if she believes your self-serving lies. I can't imagine what it would do to her if she knew you'd been playing her from the start, that she's just another source to feed your monstrous ego."

Haidar vibrated with a charge that seemed as if it would burst his every cell if it wasn't released. "And you know all about her supposed turmoil because you're her selfless confidant, right? And you want to take your so-called friendship from your squash dates into her bed. Well, hard luck. That's where I am. Constantly."

Jalal's snarl felt like an uppercut. "Very gentlemanly of you, to kiss and tell."

"No need for evasions since you know we're intimate. And still you try to take her away from me."

"You don't even want her," Jalal hissed. "You seduced her to beat me. She's just a pawn in another of your power games."

"You were the one who started *that* game, as you've conveniently forgotten."

"I forgot about that silly bet in five minutes. But you took it like you take everything, with obsessive competition. You went all out to entrap her."

"And you're out to save her from monstrous me? You're admitting you want her for yourself?"

Jalal's jaw hardened. "I won't let you use her anymore."

Rage blotched Haidar's vision. He wanted to pulverize Jalal's convictions. Arguments and defenses pummeled his mind. Then he opened his mouth and something from the repertoire of his lifelong rivalry with his closest yet furthest person came out.

A taunt. "How are you going to stop me?"

Jalal shot him a lethal glance. "I'll tell her everything."

His head almost burst.

Out of the rants clanging there, he snarled only "Good luck."

If he'd thought he'd seen antipathy in his twin's eyes before, he was wrong. *This* was the real thing. "Nothing good can come of this. You're not only like Mother—you inherited the worst of both sides of our families. You're manipulative and jealous, cold and controlling, and you have to win no matter the cost. It's time I exposed your true face to her."

Haidar's blood charred with the futility of watching this train wreck. "There's one hitch in that plan. If you do, it won't only be my face she won't want to see again, but yours, too."

"I'm okay with losing Roxanne, as long as you lose her, too."

The detonation of fury and frustration shattered his brakes. "If you tell her, Jalal, never show me *your* face again."

Bleakness spread in Jalal's eyes. "I'm okay with that, too."

A door closed, aborting the salvo of reckless bitterness he would have volleyed at his twin's intention.

Roxanne.

As she walked into the sitting room, his blood heated, his breath shortened. Her effect on him deepened with every exposure. Even when he *had* thought theirs would be a mutually satisfying liaison that would end when his fascination dissipated. Until her, he hadn't suspected himself capable of attaining such heights of emotion, plumbing such depths of passion.

She was fire made flesh, incandescent in beauty, tempestuous in spirit, consuming in power. And she was his.

He had to prove it, know it, once and for all.

The fear that she had feelings for Jalal had been compromising his sanity. His mother's passing comment about how Roxanne and Jalal shared so much had colored his view of their deepening closeness. But dread had taken root when he'd realized Roxanne had revealed the essence of her self to Jalal but not him. That had snapped his restraint, forced him to have this confrontation with both of them.

Jalal had made his position clear.

But it wouldn't matter, not if she chose *him*. As she had to.

He tried to get confirmation from the hunger that always ignited in her eyes at the sight of him. But for the second she spared him the touch of her focus, her eyes were blank. Then they swept to Jalal.

Haidar pounced on her, his fingers digging into her flesh, almost vicious in their urgency, his heart thundering. "Tell Jalal that he can't come between us no matter what he does or says. Tell him that you're mine."

Her face became a canvas of stupefaction. Then it set in hardness, her eyes becoming emerald icicles. She knocked his

hands off as if they soiled her. "That's why you so impera-
tively demanded I drop everything? How creepy can you get?"

It was his turn to gape. "Creepy? And this *is* imperative.
I've sensed Jalal developing…misconceptions about you. I
had to nip them in the bud."

Her eyes narrowed into lasers of anger and disgust. "I don't
care what you 'sensed.' You don't get to summon me as if I'm
one of your lackeys, and you can't trick me into a confrontation where you go all territorial on me and demand I parrot
back what you say. You're the one who's under the misconception that you have any claim to me."

His heart slowed to an excruciating thud, the pillars of his
mind shuddering. "I have a claim. The one you gave me when
you came to my bed, when you said you love me."

"You do remember *when* I said it, don't you?" When he'd
been arousing her to insanity and driving her to shattering or-
gasms. "But thanks for bringing things to a head. I'm going
back to the States, and I was debating how to say goodbye.
You men always take a woman walking away as a blow to
your sexual ego, and it gets messy. I was worried that it would
get extra messy with you, being the Prince of Two Kingdoms
with an ego the size of both."

His shook his head, as if from too many blows. "Stop it."

She gave a careless shrug. "Sure, let's do stop it. You were
the best candidate for the exotic fling I wanted to have while
living here. But since I decided to move back to the States,
I knew I had to end it with you. I have needs, as you know,
and no matter how good in bed you are, I'm not about to wait
until you drop by to satisfy them. I have to find a new regularly available stud. Or three. But a word of advice—don't
pull that territorial crap on *your* new women. It's really off-
putting. And it makes me unable to say goodbye with any
goodwill. Now that I know what kind of power you imagined

you had over me, I'm so turned off I don't want to ever see or hear from you again."

He watched her turn around, walk in measured steps out of the room.

In seconds the penthouse door closed with a muted thud, the very sound of rejection, of humiliation.

From the end of a collapsing tunnel he heard a macabre distortion of Jalal's voice. "What do you know? She has sharper instincts than I gave her credit for, took you only as seriously as you took her. Seems I shouldn't have worried about her."

He looked at Jalal through what felt like a stranger's eyes. "You should worry about yourself. If you ever show me your face again."

The twin he barely recognized now looked back at him with the same deadness. "Don't worry. I think it's time I detoxified my life of your presence."

Haidar stared into nothingness long after Jalal had disappeared. It wasn't supposed to happen this way.

Jalal should have told him he'd never trespass on the sanctity of his relationship with his woman. Roxanne should have denounced his doubts as ludicrous.

He should have had his twin back and his lover forever.

Those he'd thought closest to him shouldn't have walked away from him. But they had.

Trust no one.

His mother's words reverberated in his head. She'd been right.

He'd ignored her wisdom at a cost he might not survive.

Never again.

One

It wasn't every day a man was offered a throne.

When that man was Haidar, it should have been a matter of never.

But the people of Azmahar—at least, the clans that made up a good percentage of the kingdom's population—had offered just that.

They'd sent their best-spoken representatives to demand, cajole, *plead* for him to be their candidate in the race for the vacant throne of Azmahar. He'd thought they were kidding.

He'd kept his straightest face on to match their earnest efforts, pretending to accept, to brainstorm his campaign and the policy direction for a kingdom that was coming apart at the seams.

When he'd realized they were serious—*then* he'd gotten angry.

Were they out of their minds, offering him the throne of the kingdom that his closest maternal kin had almost destroyed, and his paternal ones had just dealt the killing blow? Who in

Azmahar would want him to set foot there again, let alone rule the damn place?

They'd insisted they represented those who saw him as the savior Azmahar needed.

One thing Haidar had never imagined himself as was a savior. It was a genetic impossibility.

How could he be a savior when he was demon spawn?

According to his estranged twin, he amalgamated the worst of his colorful gene pool in a new brand of bad. His recruiters had countered that he mixed the best of the lofty bloodlines running through his veins, would be Azmahar's perfect king.

"King Haidar ben Atef Aal Shalaan."

He tried the words out loud.

They sounded like a premium load of bull. Not only the "king" part. The names themselves sounded—*felt*—like lies. They no longer felt as if they indicated him. *Belonged* to him.

Had they ever?

He wasn't an Aal Shalaan, after all. Not a real one like his older brothers. Without the incontrovertible proof of their heritage stamped all over Jalal, he'd bet cries would have risen that *he* didn't belong to King Atef. From all evidence, he belonged, flesh, blood and spirit, to the Aal Munsoori family. To his mother. The Demon Queen.

The *ex*–Demon Queen.

Too bad he could never be ex–demon spawn.

His mother had besieged him from birth with her fear that her abhorred enemy, the Aal Shalaans, starting with her husband and his older sons, would taint him, the "true part" of her. She'd made sure they had no part of him. Starting with his name.

From the moment she'd laid eyes on her newborn sons, she'd seen that he was the one who was a replica of her, hadn't bothered thinking of a name for his twin. Their father had named Jalal, proclaiming him the "grandeur" of the Aal Shalaans.

Jalal was doing a bang-up job proving their father's ambitious claims right.

She'd named *him*. Haidar, the lion, one type of king. She'd been plotting to make him one that far back. When she'd known it was impossible. Through non-insurrectionist means, that was.

As a princess of Azmahar, she'd entered into the marriage of state with the king of Zohayd knowing her half-Azmaharian sons would not be in line to the throne. As per succession rules, only purely Zohaydan princes could play the game of thrones.

So she'd plotted, apparently from day one, to take Zohayd apart, then put it back together with herself in charge. She would have then been able to dictate new laws that would make her sons the only ones eligible for the throne, with him being first in line.

Two years after her conspiracy had been discovered and aborted, he still had moments when denial choked him up.

She could have caused a war. She would have, gladly, if it had gained her her objective.

She'd stolen the Pride of Zohayd jewels that conferred the right to rule the kingdom. She'd planned to give them to Prince Yusuf Aal Waaked, ruling prince of Ossaylan, so that he could dethrone her husband and claim the throne. Having only a daughter and being unable to sire another child, he would have named *her* sons his successors.

Haidar imagined she would have gone all black widow on Yusuf right after his sitting on the throne in the *joloos*, intimidated her brother—the newly abdicated king of Azmahar—into abdicating then, and put *him,* her firstborn by seven minutes, on the throne of a new superkingdom comprising Zohayd, Azmahar and Ossaylan.

She'd had such heartfelt convictions for such a heartlessly ambitious plan. When he'd pleaded with her to tell him where she'd hidden the jewels, to save Zohayd from chaos and herself from a traitor's fate, she'd calmly, *lovingly,* stated those convictions as facts.

After heavy initial damage, her plans were for the ultimate good. For who better than he to unite these kingdoms, lead them to a future of power and prosperity instead of the ruin they were heading for under the infirm hands of old fools and their deficient successors? He, the embodiment of the best of the Aal Munsooris? She was certain he'd one day surpass even her in everything.

He'd heard *that* before. According to Jalal, he already had.

But no matter what he'd thought her capable of, what she'd done had surpassed his worst predictions. And as usual, without obtaining his consent, let alone his approval, she'd executed her plans with seamless precision to force his "deserved greatness" on him. She'd been positive he'd come to appreciate what she'd done, embrace the role she'd tailored for him.

And she could have so easily succeeded.

Even Amjad, his oldest brother and now king of Zohayd, who suspected everything that moved, hadn't suspected her. As queen of Zohayd, she had seemed to have as much to lose as anyone if her husband was deposed. Ingenious.

He recognized that convoluted, long-term premeditation in his own mind and methods. But he consciously confined it to business, driving himself to the top of his tech-development and investment field in record-breaking time. His mother used her intricate intelligence with every breath.

"Please, fasten your seat belt, Your Highness."

He swept his gaze up to the flight attendant. He'd almost forgotten he was on board his private jet.

The beautiful brunette could have said, *Please, unfasten me,* for all the invitation in her eyes. She'd jump on the least measure of response in his attitude.

He regarded her with his signature impassiveness, which

had frozen hardened tycoons and brazen media people in their tracks.

Her color heightened. "We are landing."

He clicked his seat belt into place. "As I gathered."

She tried again. "Will you be needing anything?"

"La, Shokrun." He looked away, dismissing her.

Once she'd turned, he watched her undulate away, sighed.

He would order Khaleel to assign her a desk job. And to confine his immediate personnel to men, or women at least twenty years his senior.

He exhaled again, peered from his window at Durrat Al Sahel—the Pearl of the Coast—Azmahar's capital. From up here he had an eagle-eye view of the crisis he'd been called upon to wrestle with.

He'd thought he'd seen the worst of it in the oil spill off the coast. The ominous blackness tainting the emerald waters was terrible enough. But seeing the disorganization and deterioration even from this altitude was a candid demonstration of how deep the problem ran. How hard it would be to fix.

His heart tightened as the pilot started the final descent, bringing more details into sharper focus.

Azmahar. The other half of his heritage. Decaying.

What a crushing pity.

He hadn't thought he'd ever see this place again. The day Roxanne had walked out on him, he'd left Azmahar swearing he'd never return.

He wasn't only returning—he'd promised to consider the kingship candidacy. He'd made the proviso that his return would be unannounced, that he'd make his own covert investigations and reach a decision uninfluenced by more sales pitches or pleas.

He was still stunned he'd conceded that much. From all evidence, this was one catastrophic mistake in the making.

Life really had a way of giving a man reason to commit the unreasonable.

After his fatherland had rejected him, his motherland claimed to be desperate for his intervention. Investigating if he could be the one to offer it salvation was near irresistible.

He also had to admit, the idea of redeeming himself was too powerful a lure. No matter that logic separated him from his mother's treachery, the fact remained. Her actions *had* skewered into his very identity, which had already been compromised from birth by her influence. Her most outrageous transgression had tarnished his honor and image, no matter what his family said. Most of them, anyway.

Jalal had less favorable views. Of course.

Jalal. Another reason he was considering this.

His twin was another candidate for the throne, after all.

Then there was Rashid. His and Jalal's best friend turned bitterest rival. And yet another candidate.

Was it any wonder he was tempted?

Trouncing those two blowhards was an end unto itself.

So whether it was duty, redemption or rivalry that drove him, each reason was imperative on its own.

But none of them was the true catalyst that had him Azmahar-bound now.

Roxanne was.

She was back in Azmahar.

He took it as the fates nudging him to stop trying not to think of her. As he'd done for eight years. *Eight* years.

Way past high time he ended her occupation of his memories, her near monopoly of his bitterness. He had enough unfinishable business. He would lay the ghost of her share of it to rest.

He would damn well exorcise it.

"...repercussions and resolutions, Ms. Gleeson?"

Roxanne blinked at the distinguished, silver-haired man looking expectantly at her.

Sheikh Aasem Al-Qadi had been her liaison to the interim government since she'd started this post two months ago. And she had to concentrate to remember who he was, and what he—hell, what *she*—was doing here.

She cleared her throat and mind. "As you know, this affects the whole region and many intertwining international entities, each with their own complexities, interests and ideas about how to handle the situation. A rushed study would only cause more misinformation and complications."

The man raised an elegant hand adorned with an onyx-set silver ring, his refined face taking on an even more genial cast. "The last thing I intend to do is rush you, Ms. Gleeson." And if he did, he knew nothing about her if he thought an in-person nudge would make her step up her efforts. She and her team had been flat out digging in that sea. "I'm merely hoping for a more hands-on role in your investigations, and if it's available, a look at a timeline for your intended work plan."

"I assure you, you'll be the first to know when a realistic timeline can be set." She tried on the smile she'd long practiced, formal and friendly at once, which always gained her cooperation. "And my team could certainly do with the high-level insider's perspective you'd bring to the table."

After much cordiality and what she felt was a reaffirmed faith in her effectiveness, Sheikh Al-Qadi left her office.

She leaned against the door she'd closed behind him, groaned.

What *was* she doing here?

So this post *was* a politico-economic analyst's holy grail. And she *had* been bred for the role. But it had brought her back to where she could stumble upon Haidar.

She'd been certain she wouldn't. She'd kept track of him, and he'd never come back to Azmahar. And then, she was no longer the girl who'd fallen head over heels in love with him. She was one of the most sought-after analyst-strategists in

the field now, Azmahar being her third major post. If the "ax
lodged in the head," as they said here, and she did meet him,
she'd treat him with the neutrality and diplomacy of the professional that she was.

But she wouldn't have risked it if not for her mother.

When all you had in the way of family was your mother,
a word from her wielded unfair power. She hadn't stood a
chance when her mother had shed tears as she'd insisted that
this post, an expanded version of *her* old job, was *her* redemption, the perfect apology for the way *she'd* been driven from
Azmahar in shame.

When Roxanne had argued that they should have been reinstating *her,* she'd revealed she had been offered the job but
didn't want to come out of retirement. It was Roxanne who
was building her career, who was in the unique position of
possessing her mother's knowledge along with her own fresh
perspective and intrepid methods. She'd been the second on
the two-candidate shortlist for this post, and the only one with
the skill set to make a difference in it now.

She'd capitulated, signed on and packed up. And she'd been
excited. There was so much to fix in Azmahar.

According to Azmaharians, the one thing King Nedal had
done right since his *joloos* decades ago was arrange his sister
Sondoss's marriage to King Atef Aal Shalaan, winning them
Zohayd's alliance. Which had nearly been severed by Sondoss herself, the snake-in-the-grass mother of that premium
serpent, Haidar.

Roxanne had no doubt Sondoss's exile-instead-of-
imprisonment verdict had been wheedled out of the Aal Shalaans by Haidar, who could seduce the stripes off a tiger.

But when Amjad had become king, everyone had thought
the first thing he'd do was deal Azmahar the killing blow
of letting go of its proverbial hand. He hadn't owed his

ex-stepmother's homeland any mercy. Strangely enough, he hadn't ended the alliance.

Then, one month after she'd arrived, all hell had broken loose.

The arrogant fool of a now ex–crown prince had voted against Zohayd for an armed intervention in a neighboring country in the region's latest defense summit, snapping the tenuous tolerance Amjad had maintained for Azmahar. And the kingdom that had been held together by the glue of its ally's clout had come apart.

Just as Azmahar was gasping from the alienation, catastrophe struck. An explosion in one of its major oil drills caused a massive spill off its shores. Unable to deal with the upheavals, in response to the national and regional outcry, the overwhelmed and disgraced king had abdicated.

His brothers and sons, held as responsible, would no longer succeed him. Azmahar was in chaos, and Roxanne was one of those called upon to contain the situation, internally and internationally, as the most influential clans started fighting among themselves.

Out of the anarchy, consolidations had formed, splitting the kingdom into three fronts. Each backed one man for new king.

One of the candidates was Haidar.

Which meant he would come back. And she *would* stumble upon him.

She wanted that as much as she wanted a hole in the heart.

Then again, he'd already pulverized hers.

She cursed under her breath. This was ancient history, and she was probably blowing it out of proportion, anyway. She'd been a twenty-one-year-old only child who'd been sheltered into having the emotional resilience of a fourteen-year-old.

And *man,* had he been good. *Phenomenal* wouldn't do him justice.

It had only been expected that she'd gotten addicted, physically, emotionally. Then she'd woken up. End of story.

She'd moved on, had eventually engaged in other relationships. One could have worked, too. That it hadn't had had nothing to do with that mega-endowed, sizzling-blooded, frigid-hearted creature.

God. She was being cornered into defending her feelings and failures by a memory. Worse. By an illusion. Beyond pathetic.

She pushed away from the door, strode to her desk, snatched up her briefcase and purse, and headed out of the office.

It took her twenty minutes to drive across the city. One thing this place had was an amazing transportation system. Zohaydan—planned, funded and constructed.

It *would* take a miracle to pull Azmahar's fat out of the fire without Zohayd. No wonder Azmaharians were desperate to get their former ally back in their corner. And a good percentage of them had decided on the only way to do that. Put the embodiment of the Zohayd/Azmahar merger on the throne.

But as people in general were addicted to dispute, and Azmaharians were no different, they couldn't agree on which one. But disunity would serve them well now. Going after the two specimens in existence doubled their odds of having one end up on the throne.

She turned through the remote-controlled gates of the highest-end residential complex in the capital. This job came with so many perks it…unsettled her. Luxury of this level always did.

When she'd asked for more moderate accommodations, she'd been assured the project's occupancy had suffered from so many investors leaving the kingdom. They hoped her presence would stimulate renewed interest in the facility.

Seemed they'd been right. Since she'd moved in, the influx of tenants had tripled. One neighbor had told her her reputation, and her mother's, had preceded her, and her presence had many investors feeling secure enough to trickle back to Azmahar, considering it a sign things would soon be put back on track.

Yeah. Sure. *No* pressure whatsoever.

But the "privilege" she dreaded was being at ground zero with every big shot who would grace the kingdom as the race for the throne began. Word was, none of the candidates had announced a position or plans to show up. That only made stumbling across Haidar a matter of later instead of sooner.

She would give anything for never.

But then, she would give anything for a number of things. Her mother with her. A father. Any family at all.

In minutes, she was entering the interior-decorating triumph of an apartment that spanned one-quarter of the thirty-thousand-foot thirtieth floor. She sighed in appreciation as fragrant coolness and calibrating lights enveloped her.

She headed for the shower, came out grinding her teeth a bit less harshly.

She would have thrived on rebuilding the kingdom's broken political and economic channels. But now the Aal Shalaan "hybrids," as they were called here, would feature heavily in this country's future—and consequently, partly in hers. Contemplating that wasn't conducive to her focus or peace of mind. And she needed both to deal with the barrage of information she had to weave into viable solutions. Even if a new king took the throne tomorrow, and he and Zohayd threw money and resources at Azmahar, it wouldn't be effective unless they had a game plan…

An unfamiliar chime sundered the soundproof silence.

She started. Frowned. Then exhaled heavily.

Cherie was almost making her sorry she'd invited her to stay.

They'd been best friends when they'd gone to university

here, and they'd kept in touch. Roxanne's return had coincided with Cherie's latest stormy split-up with her Azmaharian husband. She'd left everything behind, including credit cards.

After the height of the drama had passed, Roxanne should have rented her a place to stay while she sorted out her affairs.

Though she loved Cherie's gregarious company, her energy and unpredictability, Cherie took her "creative chaos" a bit too far. She went through her environment like a tornado, leaving anything from clothes to laptops to mugs on the floor, dishes rotting in the sink, and she regularly forgot basic order-and-safety measures.

Seemed she'd forgotten her key now, too.

Grumbling, Roxanne stomped to the foyer, snarling when the bell clanged again. She pounced on the door, yanked it open. And everything screeched to a halt.

Her breath. Her heart. Her mind. The whole world.

Across her threshold…

Haidar.

Air clogged in her lungs. Everything blipped, swam, as the man she remembered in distressing detail moved with deadly, tranquil grace, leaned his left arm on her door frame. His gaze slid from her face down her body, making her feel as if he'd scraped every nerve ending raw, before returning to her sizzling eyes, a slow smile spreading across his painstakingly sculpted lips.

"You know, Roxanne, I've been wondering for eight years."

The lazy, lethal melody emanating from his lips swamped her. His smile morphed into what a bored predator must give his prey before he finished it off with one swat.

"How soon after you left me did you find yourself a new regularly available stud? Or three?"

Two

Something finally flickered in Roxanne's mind.

Not an actual thought. Just… *Wow.*

Wow. Over and over.

She didn't know how long it took the loop of *wows* to fade, to allow their translation to filter through her gray matter.

So *this* was what eight years had made of Haidar Aal Shalaan.

Most men looked better in their thirties than they did in their twenties. Damn them. A good percentage improved still in their forties, and even fifties. The loss of the smoothness of youth seemed to define their maleness, infuse them with character.

In Haidar's case, she'd thought there had been no room for improvement. At twenty-six he'd seemed to have already realized his potential for perfection.

But…wow. Had photographic evidence and her projections ever been misleading! He'd matured from the epitome of gorgeousness into force-of-nature-level manifestation of masculinity. Her imagination short-circuited trying to project what he'd look like, *feel* like, in another decade. Or three.

His body had bulked up with a distillation of symmetry and strength. His face had been carved with lines of untrammeled power and ruthlessness. He'd become a god of virility and sensuality, hewn from the essence of both. As harsh as the desert's terrain, as menacing as its nights. And as brutally, searingly, freezingly magnificent.

Whatever softness had once gentled his beauty, warmed the frost she'd always suspected formed his core, had been obliterated.

"Well, Roxanne?" He cocked that perfectly formed head, sending the blue-black silk that rained to his as-dark collar sifting to one side. She would have shivered had her body been capable of even involuntary reactions. She could actually hear the sighing caress of thick, polished layers against as-soft material. Mockery tugged at his lips, enhanced the slant in his eyes. He could see, feel her reaction. Of course. He was triggering it at will. "I've had bets about which of us found a replacement faster."

"Why bet on a sure thing? I had to settle in back home, re-enroll in university before I started recruiting. That took time. All *you* had to do was order a stand-in—or rather a lie-in—from your waiting list that same day."

His eyebrows shot up.

If he was surprised, it wasn't any more than she was.

Where had all that come from?

Seemed she had more resentment bottled up than she'd known. And his appearance had shaken out all the steam. Good to depressurize and get it over with.

"Touché." He inclined his head, his eyes filling with lethal humor. "I was in error. The subject of the bets shouldn't have been how long until you found replacements, but how many you found. I was just being faithful in quoting your parting words when I said a stud or three. But from…intimate knowledge of the magnitude of your...needs, I would bet you've gone through at least thirty."

Her first instinct was to take off his head with one slashing rejoinder. She swallowed the impulse, felt it scald her insides.

No matter how she hated his guts and his nerve in showing up on her doorstep, damn his incomparable eyes, he was important. Vital even. To Azmahar. To the whole damn mess. His influence was far-reaching, in the region and the world. And he had the right mix of genes in the bargain.

And then, she wasn't just a woman who was indignant to find an ex-lover at her door unannounced, but also one of the main agents in smoothing out this crisis. Whether he became king or not, he could be—*should* be—a major component in the solution she would formulate. She should rein in further retorts, drag out the professional she prided herself had tamed her innate wildness and steer this confrontation away from petty one-upmanship.

Then she opened her mouth. "By the rate *you* were going through women when I was around, you must be in the vicinity of three hundred." Before she could give herself a mental kick, the bedevilment in his smile rose, prodded her on instead. "What? I missed a zero? Is it closer to three thousand?"

He threw his head back and laughed.

Her heart constricted on what felt like a burning coal. The sound, the sight, was so merry, so magnificent, so—so... missed, even if she didn't remember him laughing like this...

"You mean 'regularly available'...um, what *is* the feminine counterpart for stud? Nymph? Siren?" He leveled his gaze back at her, dark, rich, intoxicating laughter still revving deep in his expansive chest. "But that number would pose a logistical dilemma. Even the biggest harem would overflow with that many nubile bodies. Or did you mean three thousand in sequence?"

She glared at him. "I'm sure you can handle either a con-current or a sequential scenario."

He let out another laugh. "I *knew* I should have approached you for endorsements. But I also have to burst your bubble. Whatever tales you heard of my…exploits were wildly exaggerated. I had to prioritize, after all, and other lusts took precedence. Success, power, money. The drive to acquire and sustain those doesn't mix well with deflating one's libido in a steady supply of feminine arms. And then, time is not only all of the above, it is finite. You know how time-consuming women can be."

Her lips twisted, with derision, with the twinge that still gripped her heart. "I don't. I'm still playing for the same team."

His eyes turned pseudo-amazed. "You never even…went on loan? I would have thought someone with your…needs wouldn't mind widening her horizons where the pursuit of pleasure was concerned."

"Why? Have you? Widened your horizons?"

He let out another bark of distressingly virile amusement. "How can I, when I'm a caveman who's unable to develop beyond my programming? The only thing I managed was to take your advice—purged myself of any trace of 'creepy territorial crap.'"

She reciprocated his razzing, sweeping his six-foot-five frame with disdain. By the time she came back to his eyes, she was kicking herself. It didn't do a woman's heart or hormones any good, getting a load of how his sculpted perfection filled, pushed, *strained* against his black-on-black clothes. Inviting touch, inciting madness…

She gritted her teeth against the moist heat spreading in her core. "And *that* must be the legendary eidetic memory some of you Aal Shalaans are said to possess. As if you need more blessings."

He slid an imperturbable glance down the foot between

them. "If you feel we've received more than our fair share, you can take up your grievance with the fates." A sarcastic huff accompanied a head shake. "But if you think perfect recall is a blessing, you have evidently never been plagued by anything like it. True blessing lies in the ability to forget."

Her heart squeezed with something that confused her. Regret? Sympathy? Empathy?

No. That would indicate she was responding to something *he* felt. And everyone knew that the ability to feel was not among his abilities or vulnerabilities.

She narrowed her eyes, more exasperated with the chink in her resolve than with him. "Come to think of it, it *must* be terrible to have an infallible memory. There must be so much you would have preferred to forget, or at least blur enough to rationalize and romanticize."

All traces of devilry vanished as he thrust his hands into his pockets. Her gaze dragged from his stunning face down to the silky material stretching across the potency she remembered in omnisensory detail…

"I can certainly do with some blurring to take the edge off at times." The predatory challenge flared again. "But one thing about possessing clarity that time doesn't dull—I make one hell of an unforgiving enemy, if I do say so myself."

She snorted. "Yeah. And I hear so many love you for it."

"Does it look like I'd want or even abide 'love'?"

His mock affront would have been irresistible if it wasn't also overwhelmingly goading. She felt just a second away from venting her unearthed frustration in a gnawing, clawing physical attack on this unfeeling monolith!

She exhaled. "That simpering, useless sentiment, huh? No. From what I hear, you want only obedience, blind, mute and dumb."

His smile was self-satisfaction itself. "And I get it, too. *Very* useful, and blessedly soothing, for someone in my position."

"Your mother's son to the last gene strand, aren't you?"

"I like to think I'm the updated and improved version."

His smirk made her want to drag him to her by the hair to taste those heartlessly sensual lips—and to bite them off.

Had he always been this...inflammatory?

He *had* been exasperating, unyielding in demanding his own way. And getting it. One way or another. Mainly one way. But she'd been so in love—or so in raging, blinding, enslaving lust—that the edge of fury his overriding tactics kept simmering beneath the blissful surface had only made everything she felt for him more explosive.

But now the addiction had been cured. Now that she knew what he was without a trace of the "rationalizing or romanticizing" she'd been guilty of heavily employing, she was reacting to him as she should have all along.

Yeah? With thinly suppressed hostility overlying a barely curbed resurgence of lust?

"Invite me in, Roxanne."

Her heart choked out another salvo of arrhythmia.

The electrifying invocation he made of his demand, her name.

She swallowed, trying to extricate herself from his influence, damning him and herself for how effortless it was for him, what a struggle it was for her. "You...you want to come in?"

"No, I came to conduct a verbal duel on your doorstep."

He moved forward and she surged to abort the step that would have taken him over her threshold. "I couldn't care less what you came to do. But said duel is done. Not so nice of you to drop by, Prince Aal Shalaan. Hope I don't see you again."

He resumed his former position, feet braced farther apart, hands in pockets again. "Tsk. All those reports lauding your ability to deal with the most thorny situations and the most exasperating individuals must have been exaggerated."

"No one factored you in when they were gauging thorny exasperation. Even my super diplomacy powers have a limit."

"Or maybe I'm your kryptonite." His smile was now the essence of patience. A hunter with unlimited time to set up his quarry's downfall. "As much as I enjoyed our opening skirmish out here, I would continue our battle in a more private setting. For your sake, really. You're the one who lives here. Surely you don't want your neighbors to witness our... escalations?"

"Since those won't occur, there's nothing for them to witness. Nothing but your departing back." She started to shut the door.

The polished, maple surface met a palm with two-hundred-pounds-plus of sinew, muscle and maleness behind it.

"You know who I am, right?"

Her eyes widened. "You're pulling rank?"

"You think I use my status to get my way? How boring and juvenile would that be?"

"If you're not referring to being the all-powerful Prince of Two Kingdoms, what the hell was that threat about?"

"No threat. Just statement of fact. Take all the trappings away and who am I?"

The most magnificent male in history.

Out loud she seethed. "A huge pain?"

The look he gave her had all her hairs standing on end. "The son of the queen of bitches."

She stared at him. She couldn't agree more about his mother. But she hadn't thought he had that brutal clarity about her, either, let alone would admit it.

She exhaled. "That you are."

Unperturbed, even satisfied by her agreement, his smile widened, raising the voltage of her distress. "So you realize how far I'll go to gain my objectives. Or do you need a demonstration?"

The seventy-five-hundred-square-foot apartment at her back closed in on her.

"Why is coming in even an objective? If I've aroused your confrontational beast, tell it to go back to sleep. We've used up all the digs we can make at each other. Anything else would be redundant, and neither of us likes to waste time."

His shrug was dismissal itself. "First, we're just getting warmed up. Second, surely you don't think I'll allow another abrupt ending between us? Eight years ago, you took me by surprise. *And* I was young and soft. Third, that was a rhetorical question, right? About why it's an objective to get inside... your personal space? You do look in the mirror on occasion? And you have an idea of how you look now?"

For the first time, she focused on how she must look. How she felt. Tiny and defenseless without her towering heels, business clothes and makeup, with her hair drying in a rioting jungle around her shoulders. With the added vulnerability of being just a bathrobe away from total nakedness.

She could almost feel his gaze slipping beneath the terry cloth to explore, reminisce and appraise the changes eight years had wrought in the flesh he'd once thoroughly possessed and pleasured.

Judging he'd disrupted her to the desired level, he gestured, encompassing her. "Add all *that* to the delights of your tongue of mass destruction, and you're wondering about my motives?"

She wrinkled her nose. "Quote, 'How creepy can you get,' unquote. You think I'll invite a man twice my size, twenty times as strong and two million times as powerful in every other way into my 'personal space,' after he's made his lewd intentions clear?"

His face lost all lightness. "You think you won't be safe with me?"

Haidar might be many things, but to women he would always be master through pleasure, not pain; seduction, not coercion.

Unable to get rid of him that way, she exhaled. "No. But you *are* trying to persist your way in when I don't want you here."

A smile transformed his face back to the supreme male who knew the exact level of estrogen overproduction he commanded in females. "You do. I remember, in unfailing detail, how you want, Roxanne. My knowledge of your mind may be deficient, especially with eight years of maturity and experience, but your body hasn't changed, and I know everything about it. I can sense its every nuance, decipher its every signal."

She wrestled with the overwhelming urge to knee him.

Knowledge glittered in his eyes, threatened to snap her control. "My sudden appearance rattled you. That made you defensive, and *that* made you angry. You want me to go only so you can regroup."

One little kneeing. Surely it wouldn't be too damaging. To her position.

His grin was designed to loosen her restraint another notch. "But you can get yourself together while I'm around. I'll make myself a cup of tea until you do. You can even dress if you must. If you need the fortification of clothes, that is."

"How condescending can you get?"

He inclined his head. "Condescending *is* several steps up from creepy. I must be evolving after all."

"The jury will remain out on that." He leaned more comfortably against her door frame, as if preparing to spend hours hanging around until he achieved his "objective." She looked pointedly at the foot strategically placed across the threshold. "But I still advise you to leave now. You need your beauty sleep to deal with what awaits you here. I heard you were approached for a job. The top job."

His expression remained unchanged, but she could feel

his surprise. And dismay. He had hoped that was still a secret. Why?

He finally jerked one formidable shoulder. "News still travels faster than a speeding bullet around here. As well as rumors, exaggerations and fabrications."

"This isn't any of those. It's why you're here."

His lips quirked. "And if I tell you I'm here for you?"

"I'd say that's bull. I'll also issue you further advice. My neighbors are always coming and going and receiving tons of visitors at all times. You're a famous figure, and I bet if someone sees you standing on the doorstep of a woman in a bathrobe—one who's leaving you standing there, to boot—the footage will be on the internet in minutes and will go viral in hours. Not a prudent way to start your campaign for the throne."

He pretended to worry for a moment before he grinned again. "See? You progressed to giving me strategy advice. You can do that much better when we slip into a more comfortable...environment."

She exhaled. "Very mature. Go away, Haidar."

He folded his arms over his chest. "Why?"

Why? "You want the reasons alphabetized?"

"Just pull out a random one."

"Because I want you to."

"We already established that's a false claim."

"I have no interest in what *you* established, and no intention of arguing its merit."

"Your prerogative. Mine is waiting until you give me a reason I can accept."

"Who says you have to accept anything?"

He cocked his head, his steel-dawn eyes taking on a thoughtful cast. "Still getting back at me for 'summoning you like a lackey' and daring to presume I have a 'claim' to you?"

She balled her fists. "Use that infallible memory of yours

and remember that there was nothing to get back at you for. It just…"

"Put you off. *Aih,* I remember. But you can't have been cringing ever since. And you're not doing so now. This is the very healthy reaction of the hot-blooded spitfire I was afraid had disappeared, from all reports of the imperturbable goddess of analysis and mediation you've become."

This was so unfair. That he could debate as superlatively as he did everything else. But she was no slouch in that department.

Before she could find anything to say to back up that claim, he said, "With that out of the way, repeat after me. 'It's all in the past, and will you please come in, Haidar?'"

"It's all in the past, and will you please go away, Haidar?"

He unfolded his arms, braced his hands on his hips. "You think it's a possibility I will? I'm beginning to lose faith in the clarity of your insight and the accuracy of your projections."

She gritted her teeth. Exchanging barbs was like quicksand. The more she said, the further she sank. She'd say no more.

He gave her one last brooding glance. Then he turned around.

He—he was…leaving?

She watched him walk away, got a more comprehensive view of his…assets as he receded. Just looking at him had longing clamping her chest.

He was messing with her. Haidar didn't give up. He didn't know how.

But he was now at the far end of the hall that led to the elevators. He was really leaving.

Before he made the left that would take him out of sight, he stopped. Her heart revved a jumble of beats. Would he…?

He turned, rang the bell of her farthest neighbor.

What the hell…?

Without stopping, he continued retracing his steps, stopped

by the second-farthest apartment, ringing its bell, too. With-out slowing down this time, he did the same at her closest neighbor's.

Then he moved to the middle of the hall, semifacing her, calmly sweeping his gaze across all the doors.

Before his actions could sink in, one door opened. Two seconds later, another did. The last followed.

Then her neighbors—and, just her luck, the female compo-nents only—stood staring at Haidar. Their wariness at having their bells rung without a preceding intercom alert turned to amazement as recognition dawned.

Haidar let them marinate in it before he said, "Sorry for dis-turbing you, ladies. I wasn't sure which apartment I wanted."

Roxanne's jaw dropped. Or dropped farther. Where had that accent come from? He sounded like a redneck!

"Oh, my *God!* You're him!" Susan Gray, the forty-something CEO of the Azmaharian branch of a multinational construc-tion company, babbled like a teenager. "You're Prince Haidar Aal Shalaan!"

Haidar shook his regal head, making his mane undulate in a swish of silk—on purpose, she was sure. "Oh, I'm just his doppelgänger. I was paid five grand online by some lady who wants to act out her fantasy of dominating him. I usually come for less, but I charged extra since she wants to get real kinky. I was given this address, the floor, but not the number of the condo. So which of you has a thing for this Haidar guy?"

Her neighbors gaped at him, at each other, then finally, at her. She was the one in the bathrobe, after all.

Her brain was too zapped to function. But she had to. If she didn't do something, this…this…*madman* would demol-ish her image. And his own.

She staggered out of her apartment, her perspiring bare feet making her advance on the polished marble precarious.

He watched her with feigned uncertainty. "Oh, it's you?"

His gaze swept her with what looked like earnest assessment. "I somehow thought you wouldn't be a babe. So why can't you find guys to dominate the regular way? Hey…you're not nuts, are you?"

He looked to her neighbors for confirmation as she stumbled the last step to him, grabbed him by the lapel of his jacket.

He pretended to ward her off. "Whoa, lady. The deal is degradation in private. Public displays will cost you extra."

She grimaced at her neighbors, expending all her restraint on not thumping the huge lout. "Sorry, ladies. Haidar is an old friend, regretfully. I left him eight years ago without a sense of humor, but it seems he's contracted some terminal prankster disease. He thinks this is a fun way to say long time no see."

She was dragging him toward her apartment while she talked, for the second time in her life wishing grounds yawned open and swallowed people. The other time had also involved him.

He resisted her, looked back at her neighbors imploringly. "I don't know this dame. Is she dangerous?" She smacked him hard on the arm. "Hey! We agreed on domination, not abuse!"

The son of a literal royal bitch was making the situation worse with every word out of his mouth.

Who was she kidding? It was irretrievable already. *God.*

She could think of nothing to say but "Shut up, Haidar."

He looked down at her, eyes morphing from vapid porn-actor mode to a dozen devils' cunning. "I'm a working dude, lady. Show me some respect. When I'm not on the clock, that is."

Her neighbors' expressions kept yo-yoing from the verge of bursting into laughter to wondering if their neighbor did have a kinky—or worse—side to her.

"You win, okay?" she grumbled for his ears only. "Now stop with the act, take your bows and let the ladies get on with their evening."

He raised his voice for all to hear. "So you'll pay extra if I start pretending I'm this Haidar guy right now?"

"*Ooh!*" She shoved him ahead of her across her threshold.

This time he surrendered to her manhandling, clung to the edge of the door, addressed them over her head. "Do you mind checking up on me in an hour's time?"

She shot her flabbergasted neighbors another dying-of-embarrassment glance, dragged him away from the door, slammed it shut.

Then she rounded on him.

His grin lit up his impossibly gorgeous face. "I did warn you. Next time, give in gracefully."

She stomped her heel over his foot. It felt like ramming rock-enclosed steel. Pain shot through her whole leg, had her hopping on one foot yelping.

He caught her by the arms, steadied her, chuckling. "Go put on your most lethal stilettos and we'll try it again."

Grimacing, she punched his chest, hard. "You reckless jerk."

He groaned, definite pleasure darkening the deep, rich sound.

So the bastard hadn't been lying about his predilections after all. The savage, dominating edge to his desire used to thrill her. But maybe he didn't mind exchanging roles. Something to keep in mind…

The trajectory of her thoughts made her whack him again.

He bit his lip with what looked like intense enjoyment, his eyes sparkling like turbulent seas in a full moon. "Is that the political adviser's indignation? How sweet of you to care."

"I care about *my* effectiveness. As for you, by the time this gets out, and boy will it, you can kiss the throne goodbye."

"Fair enough. As long as I can finally kiss you hello."

He dragged her up until only her toes touched the hardwood floor, swooped his head down to hers and did just that.

At the first touch of his lips, she spiraled like a shot-down plane into the past. All her being was captured into a reenactment of that first kiss that had swept her away on a tide of addiction. He took her mouth with that same lazy savoring laced with coiled ferocity. Her body had learned then what kind of heart-stopping pleasure such deceptively patient coaxing would lead to, had burst into flames at his merest touch, fire raging higher with each exposure.

The conflagration was fiercer now, with the fuel of anger, of eight years of repression. This was wrong, insane. And it only made her want it, want him, more than her next breath.

Gravity loosened its hold on her, relinquished her to the effortless levitation of his arms. The world spun in hurried thuds, then she was sinking into the firmness of a couch as his weight sank over her. Her moans rose, confessions of the arousal that had fractured the shackles of hostility and memory and logic, drowned them and her.

The rough heat of him electrified her as her bathrobe and his shirt came undone. His chiseled, roughened steel flesh crushed her swollen breasts, teasing her turgid nipples into a frenzy. His bulk and power settled between her spread thighs, and he ground against her molten core, plunged into her gasping mouth.

She writhed to accommodate him, enfold him, the decadence of him on her tongue, lacing her every sense.

Suddenly he severed their meld. She cried out as he rose above her. His gaze scalded her, his lips tight with grim sensuality.

"I should have listened to what my body knows about yours and done this the moment you opened the door."

His arrogance should have made her buck him off. But lust gnawed her, ruled her. Hunger for him, as he was now, memorized yet unknown, the same yet changed beyond compre-

hension, brimming with contradictions, seethed its demand
for satisfaction.

He'd come here for this possession, this closure. She'd been
aching for it, too. She's only be hurting herself if she denied—

A slam sent the crystal on the mahogany table beside them
emitting a harmony of hums, felt like being drenched in ice
water.

Cherie.

"You won't believe who I found waiting for me. Ayman in
all his glory, wanting to talk. Why now, I ask you…"

Cherie's prattling trailed off. Roxanne met her eyes over
Haidar's shoulders, would have giggled at her friend's deer-in-
the-headlights expression if she weren't as distressed.

If Cherie had been any later, Haidar would have been buried deep inside her, thrusting her to oblivion.

Even now, with horror at her actions crashing over her, her
body still whimpered for his completion.

"Cherie…" was all she could wheeze.

"Uh…I… God, I didn't mean—" Cherie stopped, before
spluttering again, "I never thought you'd…you'd…"

She'd never thought she'd find her cerebral friend beneath
a lion of a man, naked and wrapped around him, in full view
for her to see as soon as she walked in the door.

Haidar began to rise off her. She stared up into his face
as it changed from ferocious lust to deprecating resignation.

"A flatmate, Roxanne? Seriously?"

"What am I *doing* still standing here?" Cherie babbled as
she ran inside. "Sorry, guys. Please, carry on. I'm not really
here!"

By the time they heard Cherie's bedroom door slam, he
was on his feet, buttoning his shirt. For one mad moment, she
didn't see why they couldn't take Cherie's advice.

Then sanity lodged back into her brain.

She scrambled up, pulled her bathrobe tight around her.

He shook his head at her far-too-late modesty as he turned away.

At the door, he half turned again, his eyes hooded with still-simmering desire. "We'll meet again, *ya naari.*"

She lurched. *His fire.*

She'd never thought she'd hear that again. From him. Or ever. She'd long thought her fire had been extinguished.

"But next time, it will be on my turf. And on my terms."

He touched his tongue to the lip she'd bitten, as if tasting her passion. Then, with one last inflaming look, he whispered, "Until then."

Three

"I'd give an arm to know your secret, Roxanne."

Roxanne stared at Kareemah Al Sabahi. Hers was the third and last door she'd knocked on to explain away Haidar's shenanigans.

She hadn't been up to facing another day, let alone those who'd witnessed Haidar's innovative blackmail tactics. But damn him to an as-novel hell, she had to live among them, as he'd said.

Kareemah was the only one who hadn't needed explanations, having watched developments through her intercom camera. Cherie's arrival had had her mind going into hyperdrive. But Haidar had left minutes later, aborting her visions of threesomes. She'd opened her door, hoping for an explanation, when he'd suddenly turned. In his real voice, he'd said he hoped she'd enjoyed the show, had her giggling like a fool as he'd bowed to her before he'd walked away.

"I mean, you're gorgeous and all, but it can't only be that. You have to have a secret. Women everywhere would kill for a tip."

Roxanne shook her head. She wasn't up to deciphering

neighbors' riddles. Now that Haidar had rematerialized in her life with the force of a live warhead and left promising further destruction, her brain was officially fried.

Either that, or Kareemah was talking gibberish. Which was an imminent possibility. The woman *had* been exposed to Haidar, too.

"So what *do* you do to get gods knocking down your door?"

"Uh, Kareemah, if you mean Haidar, I already explained—"

"And I might have bought you explaining one god away. But how do you explain another?"

Suddenly, she realized Kareemah wasn't looking at her. Her eyes were glued to a point in the distance.

Someone was standing behind her.

She whirled around. And her heart hit the base of her throat.

No. Not another Aal Shalaan "hybrid."

Jalal.

He was standing by the door she'd left open, in a charcoal suit with a shirt the color of his golden eyes, hands languidly in his pockets, looking as if he'd teleported off a *GQ* magazine cover.

That might not be far-fetched. She hadn't heard the whir of the elevator or the fall of his footsteps.

For the second time in less than twenty-four hours, one of the two men she never wanted to see again had managed to sneak up on her.

Kareemah tugged on her arm, made her stagger around. "Like we say here, 'the neighbor takes precedence in charity.' I anxiously await a glimpse at your methods."

With that, she cast Jalal another starstruck glance and stepped back into her apartment.

Roxanne stared at the door Kareemah had just closed, her mind in a jumble.

"*Koll hadi's'seneen, kammetman'nait ashoofek menejdeed.*" All these years, how I wished to see you again.

Her heart squeezed so hard she felt it would implode.

Suddenly fury spurted inside it, incinerating all shock and nostalgia. She wasn't letting another Aal Shalaan twin mess her up all over again. She'd hit her limit last night.

She turned, hoping she didn't look as shaky as she felt. "If it isn't one of the region's two most eligible bastards."

The warmth infusing his face didn't waver as he slipped his hands out of his pockets, spread his arms in a gesture that had always had her running into them. "*Ullah yehay'yeeki, ya* Roxanne."

Ullah yehay'yeeki—literally, may God hail you, one of the not-quite-translatable colloquial praises he'd once lavished on her, usually when she'd said something that had resonated with his demanding intellect and wit. Which had been almost every time she'd opened her mouth. They'd been so alike, so in tune, it had been incredible. It had also turned out to be a lie.

For years afterward, she hadn't known which betrayal had hurt more, his or Haidar's.

She stuck her fists at her sides. "Listen, buddy, I had one hell of a night, and I'm expecting a spiral of steady deterioration for the foreseeable future. So why don't you just piss off. Whatever made you pop up here, I don't want to hear it."

"Not even if it's me groveling for forgiveness?"

She walked toward him, each step intensifying her anger. "I've heard that before. Still not in the least interested."

He'd called her out of the blue two years ago, begging her for a face-to-face meeting. She'd hung up on him.

He hadn't called back.

She came to a stop a foot away, had to still look way up, even when boosted by her highest heels.

In response to her glare, he did something that made her heart stagger inside her chest. He cupped her cheek, his touch the essence of gentleness, his face, his voice that of cherishing.

"*Alhamdu'lel'lah*—thank God the years have been as

nurturing as you deserve. You've grown into a phenomenal woman, Roxy."

Only the drowning wave of longing stopping her from scoffing, *Look who's talking.*

Jalal was another case where time had conspired to turn an example of virile perfection into something that was description defying. While the younger man she'd known had been as gorgeous as she'd thought humanly possible, possessing an equal, if totally different, brand of beauty from his twin and a diametrically opposite effect, too, the mature Jalal had become a juggernaut out of an Arabian Nights fable.

"Even if you scratch my eyes out for it, you have to hear it, to know it. *Kamm awhashtini, ya sudeequtti al habibah.*" How I missed you, my beloved friend.

And *God*, how she'd missed him, too.

She grabbed his hand, removed it from her face, tugged him by it. He let her lead him, offering no resistance even when it became clear she was taking him to the elevators.

In seconds, an elevator swished silently open. She gestured for him to enter. With one last pained, resigned look, he complied. And she made up her mind.

She dragged him back out, led him to her apartment.

She let him close the door, walked ahead to her spacious home office, threw herself down on the L-shaped cream leather couch/recliner, looked up at him as he came to stand before her.

She made a hurry-up gesture. "Go ahead. Grovel. Just try to make it interesting."

His expression turned whimsical. "That will be hard. Will you accept pathetic?"

"I'm sure it will be that."

He sighed, nodded. "But I want to make sure of something first. That day—you arrived before you made your presence known, right? You overheard me and Haidar talking about our bet?"

He was only half right about how it had happened. She wasn't about to volunteer more insights. "What do you think?"

"I think it's the only explanation for what you said and did. Even if you were angry with Haidar for his overbearing tactics, even if you'd told the truth about the limit of your involvement with him, you had no reason to cut me off, too. Except if you heard. And misinterpreted what you heard."

Heat rose as she relived the humiliation and heartbreak all over again. "Don't even try the misinterpretation card. What I heard was the truth, and I acted accordingly to get rid of both of you competition-sick bastards. End of story."

Her insults had no effect on him. Just as they hadn't on Haidar.

But while Haidar had been bedeviling and goading, Jalal was accepting and forbearing. He'd let her beat him to a pulp if it would make her feel better.

"You of all people know there are too many sides to any situation for one to be the whole truth."

But she *didn't* want to hear more sides to this mess. Hope was more damaging than resignation. She'd built her stability around accepting the worst, dealing with the pain and moving on.

But…hadn't she spent years wishing there *were* more sides? Ones that might prove that not everything they'd shared had been a means to a "pathetic" end, so she could free a measure of her memories from the pall of bitterness and resentment?

His wolf's eyes felt as if they were probing her mind, following her every thought. Which they probably were. They'd always been on the same wavelength.

Just as the scales teetered toward foolish hope, his gaze grew relieved. He *was* reading her like a hundred-foot billboard.

"Will I get socked if I sit down beside you?"

She flung him an ill-tempered gesture. "Take your chances like the colossal man that you are."

He sat down inches away with controlled strength and poise, cocooning her in warmth and power and a nostalgia so encompassing her throat closed.

She took refuge in sarcasm. "This couch is so low most people flop down on it. Still doing thousands of squats per day?"

"Takes one exercise junkie to know another. You're looking fitter than ever, Roxy." Before she hissed that he'd lost the right to call her that, he silenced her with something totally unexpected. "I need to explain something I should have long ago. My relationship with Haidar."

Her heart blipped in distress at Haidar's name. At the way Jalal said it. At the bleakness in his eyes.

She attempted a nonchalant shrug. "While neither of you ever talked about the other, I gathered the relevant facts myself. You live to compete with each other."

"Aren't you at all curious to know how we got that way?"

"Standard sibling rivalry, how else? As you said, pathetic. But most of all, boring."

"How I wish it was. Maddening, unsolvable, heart-wrenching more like." He wiped a hand down his face in a weary gesture. "You've seen how radically different we are, and we were born that way. But we were inseparable in spite of that. Maybe because of it. Until it all started going wrong. I can trace the beginning of the friction, the rivalry, to one incident. Our tenth birthday party."

Here was her first misconception destroyed. She'd always assumed their rivalry started at birth.

"I almost burned down the palace, and Haidar volunteered to take the blame. Instead of stepping forward, I…let him take the punishment meant for me. Things were never the same afterward."

Their conflict had an origin, one in which Haidar was the wronged party? That *was* surprising. Disturbing.

"He began to treat me with a reserve I wasn't used to, put distance between us. Once I became certain it wasn't a passing thing, I was furious, then anxious, then lost. I needed my twin back. I tried to force the closeness I depended on, dogging his every move, demanding to share everything he did, for him to share everything I did, like we used to. When that only resulted in more distance, I became desperate. I started to do anything that would provoke an emotional reaction from him. He retaliated by demonstrating in ingenious ways that I couldn't get to him. Then he learned a new trick, wielded a new weapon—he started showing me, and everyone else, that he was better than me. In just about everything. And it was so easy for him.

"He got the highest grades without trying, while I had to struggle to keep up. He was a favorite with our elders for being so methodical and achieving. He was a sweeping success with girls for being so good-looking, yet so cool and detached. The only thing I could trounce him in was sports, and he came close to equaling me even in those by mere cunning."

He gave a deprecating laugh. "And of course, all through, our mother was praising the hell out of his every breath. As a boy who then idolized his mother, I grew frantic for equal appreciation, and when I despaired of that, for any at all. She did show me some on occasion, but it always felt like the crumbs that were left over from Haidar's feast. It took me years to outgrow the need for her validation, to be resigned to who she was, and the kind of relationship I had with her. But I could never become resigned to my and Haidar's relationship.

"It was a paradox. I wanted to be with him the most of anyone in the world, yet no one could drive me out of my cool, collected mind but him…at least, no one *then*…" A dark, distracted look settled in his eyes. Before she could ask who else had later done the same to him, he shook his head slightly as if to rid himself of disturbing memories, resumed his focus. "He seemed to want my company as much, in his own contradictory way, showing me moments of emotional closeness before shutting me out again."

You, too? she almost scoffed. Haidar had subjected her to the same dizzying, confusing, addicting pattern.

Jalal sat back, fists braced on his knees, eyes seeming to gaze into his own past. "As we got older, we showed the world a unified front, for the sake of the rest of our family, politics and business. But when we were alone, we butted heads like two stupid rams on steroids. And I think we both were addicted to the conflict. I believed that was who we were, the only relationship we could have, and I had to accept it."

Roxanne gaped at his grim profile. She'd never thought things were that complex and complicated between them. It was fascinating in the most terrible way to learn how these two twins who had everything they needed to forge an unparalleled bond had been driven apart. Needing to reach out to each other yet held back by something inescapable.

And *why* was she including them both in that assessment? She'd bet Haidar felt no equal anguish for the state of affairs with his twin. She'd bet Haidar didn't feel at all.

But where Jalal was concerned, so much now made sense. The wistfulness and guardedness that had come over him when Haidar was mentioned, the snarkiness that took over when his twin was around.

No matter if this snowball had started with an incident in which Jalal was the culprit—that Haidar had set out to punish his twin for it for the rest of their lives proved what a twisted, vindictive bastard he was. He'd even been proud of the fact that he made one hell of an unforgiving enemy.

Jalal threw his head back on the couch. "But accepting it didn't mean I could handle it. Being unreasonable isn't part of my makeup, but I became that with Haidar. And I no longer knew how much of our rivalry was due to what had turned him against me early on, or to my self-defeating tactics in trying to get him back, our mother's divisive influence, or who we are, our choices, actions and reactions. Then we met you at that royal ball."

Her heart did its best to flip over inside her rib cage.

How she remembered that night.

It had been in her first month in Azmahar. She'd thanked the fates for the job that had gotten her mother and herself here. When they were invited to that ball, she'd felt like a Disney heroine entering a world of wonders way beyond her wildest dreams. The impression had grown stronger when she'd met Jalal.

Then she'd seen Haidar.

Just the sight of him, an apparition of aloof, distant grandeur, had kicked to life every contradictory emotion inside her. She'd bristled with defensiveness, burned with challenge and melted with desire.

Jalal turned to her now, taking his account from the profoundly personal to the shared past. "I saw your instant attraction to him, and out of habit, I challenged him for you. We both know how far he took that challenge. But I swear to you, I forgot that silly bet in minutes. Everything you and I shared was real. You were the friend I could share everything with, the sister I never had."

And he'd been her confidant, champion and the brother she'd always longed for.

Still afraid of reopening her heart and letting him seal the hole losing him had blown in it, she narrowed her eyes. "So why did you wait six years to approach me? And even then, give up after just one phone call?"

"Because after you walked out and didn't call me, I assumed you'd overheard us and included me in your hostility. My first impulse was to run to you, tell you what I just told you now. But as I was heading out to your house the next morning, I learned that your mother had been…dishonorably discharged. I held back then because I believed further contact with me might cause you more…damage."

She blinked her surprise. "Why did you think that?"

"Didn't you ever suspect why your mother was fired?"

"Sure I did. I suspected Haidar."

It was his turn to be shocked. "You thought he was punishing you for walking out on him through her?"

"You find that far-fetched?"

He clearly did, found her suspicion very disturbing. "I prefer to think there are some lines he wouldn't cross."

"You think seducing me for a bet was an okay line to cross, but destroying my mother's career to get back at me wasn't?"

"I…" He drove his fingers into his sable mane in agitation. "I guess it's not impossible, considering he must have been enraged at the time, but it just doesn't…feel like him."

"So if it wasn't Haidar you were worried would harm us more if you maintained a relationship with me, who were you afraid of?"

"My mother." He grimaced when her jaw dropped. "I don't have proof, but I felt her hand in this. She employed similar tactics to drive those she didn't approve of away from Haidar and me. Again, I never found proof, but I just *knew* she was behind all those incidents. That's why I ventured to contact you only when she was exiled. Until then, there was no telling how far she'd go if she learned you were still in my life."

She gaped at him. This was a scenario she hadn't considered. Not because she didn't have the worst possible opinion of former queen Sondoss. But she'd thought the queen had already been done with her, had no more reason to go after her or her own.

Then again, knowing that woman, why not?

Could it be? All these years she'd been so busy demonizing Haidar, she'd missed the mother of all demons at work?

Feeling her entrenched convictions being uprooted, leaving her in a free fall of new confusion, she released a tremulous breath. "You've got yourself one effed-up family, Jalal."

"Tell me about it."

She teetered on the verge of throwing herself into his arms and hugging the despondency out of him.

One more thing first. "So why didn't you persist, after your mother was out of the picture and I was no longer in her range?"

His look of self-blame almost made her stop him from answering. "Because I was going through some…heavy stuff, with Haidar, with…other people, and I acutely felt the kind of anger and hurt that could fuel your hanging up on me after six years. I thought I'd be a reminder of your worst memories after you'd moved on. I was also not in any shape to take more emotional upheavals at that time."

Her hands fisted on the urge to reach out. "What's changed?"

"You did." His golden eyes blazed with pride and fondness so powerful and pure, hers started burning. "You came back. It proved to me you're ready to face your demons, to snatch what you deserve from their fangs. I now think having me back in your life won't resurrect painful memories—you're ready to remember the good ones and form new and better ones. And I have also changed. I'm removed enough from my 'effed-up' family that I can be your haven again. *And* the big gun in your camp."

The tears she'd been holding back for eight years cascaded down her cheeks. He reached for her as she did him, took her into his long-missed affection and protection.

He kissed the top of her head. "Does this mean you believe me?"

She raised a face trembling with mirth and emotion. "What else could it mean, you big, wonderful wolf?"

"That you're too softhearted, that you forgive me even if you still believe I befriended you to seduce you away from Haidar."

She smirked, poked her finger into that dimple in his left cheek. "As if you could have seduced me. Or even wanted to."

His smile was relief itself. "*Aih,* I would have found Haidar's accusations hilarious, if I hadn't been so incensed with him. You felt like my real twin from the first time we met, *ya azeezati.*"

A sob escaped her at hearing him call her "my dearest" again. "You don't know how much I missed you...*ya azeezi.*"

"That's it?" he mock reprimanded her. "You're taking me back into your heart? And I'd hoped you'd grown as diamond-hard as the exterior you project. You still have a gooey center."

She knew what he was doing. He was taking this away from acute emotions, even if the positive, wonderful variety. "Takes one mushy core to know another." She jumped to her feet, dragged him up with both hands. "I didn't have breakfast yet. Share it?"

His grin lit up the whole world. "Sure will. I haven't eaten a thing since yesterday, dreading this confrontation."

"Says the man who once went swimming with sharks."

"*Azeezati,* first, that was for a zillion dollars in donations for your list of causes. Second, your possible rejection—and worse, my inability to heal your pain—were far scarier propositions than being gnawed on by sharks."

She kissed him soundly on the cheek for that.

For the next hour, they talked and laughed and shared news and opinions as if they'd never stopped. It felt like being in the past, when she'd raced through her work so she could run to her squash date whenever he was in the kingdom.

They were sipping mint tea when he said, "Apart from being my friend and sister again, I need your professional services."

One eyebrow rose. "Uh-oh. This *was* too good to be true."

"You think all this—" he gestured to their cozy companionship "—was me leading up to this request?"

It took her a moment to make up her mind. "I might be a colossal fool with syrup for blood, but no. I trust you too much."

"You didn't trust me at all till a couple of hours ago."

She shook her head. "That's not true. Even if I didn't hear you defending me to Haidar, I would have believed that however things started, the feelings you developed for me were genuine. It was because I thought you cut me from your life that I developed a grudge against you. I missed your friendship sometimes more than I missed the illusion of my love for Haidar."

He dragged her into his arms for a convulsive hug. "I can't tell you sorry I am, how angry I am for the heartache my family caused you and forced me to be party to inflicting on you." He set her away, held her by the shoulders. "But I will never let anyone hurt you again." She nodded, a tear slipping down her face. He wiped it away gently. "This means you'll consider my request?"

She mock shoved him. "Without knowing specifics, I have to remind you that friends and business are never a good mix."

"Usually not, but not *never*. When it's the right people, the right friendship, results can be spectacular. And lifelong."

"There *have* been recorded incidents." She faced him, folding her legs on the couch. "Okay. What do you propose?"

He mirrored her position. "With your connections, you must have heard I was approached by four of Azmahar's major clans to be their candidate for the throne."

"I *was* asked to weigh in on candidates. You, Rashid Aal Munsoori and…Haidar are the ones who made it to the final round."

He couldn't have missed her hesitation over Haidar's name, but made no comment. "I want you to be my consultant, my all-round adviser. I am ambivalent about this whole thing, and I need the guidance of someone I trust implicitly, someone neutral, who knows all the goings-on of the political and economic scene. Is there anyone else on the planet you know who fits the bill?"

"With those criteria, no." She chewed her lip. "Though I must qualify your 'neutral' assertion."

His head shake was adamant. "What you lack in neutrality, you'll make up for in professionalism."

"Vote of confidence appreciated and all, but…" She took a deep breath, admitted, "This will put me in contact with… him."

"If that's your objection, then my quest is done. Haidar and I will probably not be in each other's vicinity in this lifetime."

Her heart missed a beat. "It's that bad?"

"I haven't talked to him in two years."

That *was* bad. But… "You were always 'not talking to each other.' Then you'd end up drawn back together like magnets."

"I thought so, too. I left him that day eight years ago with the agreement that we were getting the hell out of each other's lives. But we were drawn back together, over and over. During the crisis in Zohayd, it seemed we were back to being as close as we were as children. Then—" a spasm contorted his noble features "—we clashed again. The last time we met, he renounced our very blood tie."

Her heart quivered, her lungs burned. If their bond had been truly severed this time, Jalal must be bleeding internally.

As for Haidar, his reptilian genes no doubt protected him from injury. The man who'd goaded, manipulated and almost seduced her out of her mind hadn't been suffering from anything.

She drew in a ragged inhalation. "Okay, I'll do it. But I'll make sure that there is no conflict of interest with my job, and I won't divulge anything that would provide you with any unfair advantage, just sort your own findings and add my own insights. And of course I would be helping you on a strictly informal, personal basis, not officially."

She didn't know if he was more relieved that she'd accepted, or that she'd made that stipulation. Seemed he, too, was still considering Haidar and his reactions in everything he did.

That was a reason unto itself to see Jalal to the throne.

She'd be saving a whole kingdom from having Haidar as king.

Four

"How far are you willing to go for her?"

Haidar blinked, unable to turn his gaze from the second most magnificent sight he'd ever seen.

It was downright...magical. The undulating shore hugging pristine, placid aquamarine that in turn tugged at its unique red-gold edge in a tranquil, laced-in-delicate-froth dance. The bay that sent a tendril of land to almost touch the island teeming with palm trees just half a mile away. The canopy of crisp azure adorned in brushstrokes of incandescent white. Every wisp of breeze, every whiff of fragrance, every ray of light... breathtaking.

And he'd thought nothing could take his breath away anymore.

Seemed instead of becoming harder as he grew older, he was getting softer. A tiny, barefoot woman in a bathrobe had done just that last night. Taken it away, and held it at bay with her every move. And this place felt like an echo of...

"Her?"

He repeated the word as his eyes fell on his much smaller, middle-aged companion. He kept forgetting he was there.

The man, overdressed for the time and climate, beamed. "The estate. In the real estate business, everyone refers to it as 'her.' Comes from dozens of men going to lengths to acquire it that are normally reserved for bewitching and out-of-reach women."

He could see how. He'd gone driving last night after he'd left Roxanne, and he'd registered nothing until he'd happened by this place.

He'd parked at the top of the dune that overlooked it, watched it transition through the grandeur of a starlit canvas to the glory of a majestic dawn to that of a sun-drenched morning. That he could appreciate any of it while he wrestled with his need to tear his way back to Roxanne proved this place was phenomenal indeed.

But as he'd sat there suffering, it had become clear to him.

He wanted her. And he would have her. Here.

He'd called Khaleel with his GPS coordinates, told him he would buy this place. In less than an hour the real estate agent had arrived, drooling at the prospect of a record-breaking deal.

They were standing at the ground-level terrace surveying the house that looked like a cross between a huge tent and a sail ship.

"...as you've seen, apart from the unique location and natural assets of this place, the house itself is a miracle of design. All bedrooms suites, sitting areas, upper and lower kitchens, formal and informal dining rooms have a sea view. Everything is arranged in an exquisite amalgam of Ottoman and Andalusian summer courtyard style, with waterways and gardens nestled within the interior—"

"As I have seen." Haidar interrupted the slick Elwan Al-Shami's sales pitch. He'd let him take him through the place, even though he'd already seen it as he'd waited for his arrival. The estate's caretakers had fallen over themselves to show him around as soon as they'd recognized him. "Let's close the deal."

The man's eyes brimmed with eagerness, yet Haidar could see he wasn't ready to do so yet. He was programmed to keep driving a client's acquisition need to fever pitch before he sprang the killing price. Even now that Haidar had made his efforts redundant, he couldn't stop before his program had run through.

"When the owner heard it was you, he named a too-exorbitant figure. That's why I asked how far you're willing to go."

Haidar swept his gaze around the place that answered any visions of heaven he'd ever had. "Shrewd man. He knows it would sell no matter how high he goes."

"And he demands cash. That's why those who bought it before fell behind in paying the installments of the huge loans they took, had to relinquish it to the indebting banks. The owner was always there to buy it back and make a profit."

"He won't be buying it back this time."

"As long as you're sure—"

"*B'Ellahi ya rejjal.* Name your price."

The man blinked at Haidar's growl. Then licking his lips nervously, he did.

Haidar whistled. No wonder many men had been broken by their desire to acquire this place.

Just as the man started to look worried, Haidar gestured to the distance. "Throw in those dunes and the land up to the road and you have a deal. Send me the contract and payment details. I want this finalized by tomorrow morning."

Before the man could express his elation at this once-in-a-lifetime deal, Haidar waved goodbye and headed to his car.

As he drove away, he took one more turn around the area to soak in the sight of the place that would be his in hours. It already felt as if it had always belonged to him.

He could have gotten it at half the asking price.

But this haven of solace and seclusion was worth the expense. It hadn't felt right to haggle for something he appreciated this much.

And then, he had to save bargaining powers for what lay ahead.

The war of reacquiring Roxanne.

Haidar's body now officially hated "Cherie."

If it sustained lasting damage from the blow of deprivation her sudden appearance had dealt it, it would remember her as his worst enemy.

Nothing was working to mitigate the gnawing need for Roxanne. Not even bringing himself to release twice while mentally reenacting their plummet into sensual delirium, this time to an explosive end.

He'd continue to ache until he slaked his hunger in her body. At least three times a day. For a month. To start.

He rested his forehead against the wet marble as he let the barrage of cold, needle-sharp water pelt his flesh, attempt to put out the inferno she'd relit inside him.

And to think he'd sought her out to prove that he'd blown her effect on him out of proportion. That he'd find the older edition of the woman who'd dealt him his life's harshest humiliation and disillusion hard and off-putting. And that gaping hole in his psyche would be sealed once and for all.

Then he'd seen her. Talked to her. Dueled with her. Touched her. Fast-forward to his current agony.

Way to exorcise the memory of her, you idiot.

Instead, he'd only managed to resurrect it to full raging life. Worse. He'd managed to create a new breed of monster. An insatiable one that nothing would appease except total and repeated satisfaction of its every craving.

He had to give it everything it hungered for.

Not that she'd make it easy. Not that he'd want her to.

Sure, she'd melted at his touch, would have let him take everything he wanted, taken everything he gave. But he had no illusions. That surrender wouldn't be repeated. For some reason, she was averse to letting him back into her bed. Perhaps the career woman she was wanted her men safe and convenient, when he was anything but. Or she feared indulging her lust would compromise her career. Whatever it was, the element of surprise had been expended. All he had now was post-almost-sex upheaval.

He had to strike again while the iron was white-hot.

He exited the shower cubicle, didn't bother drying anything but his hands, strode across the hotel suite to his cell phone.

He dialed her number, gritted his teeth as he waited for her to pick up.

She would. Because she wouldn't recognize his number.

"Hello?"

He squeezed his eyes. *Aih*. It hadn't been temporary insanity. If one breathy hello could have him fully hard all over again, she now operated his hormonal controls.

His lips twitched in self-deprecation at his weakness, in satisfaction at intending to give in to it thoroughly.

"Is Cherie gone?"

The silence that greeted his question indicated that it had stopped her breathing. Good. He shouldn't be the only one having trouble breathing over this thing between them.

"I can come over if she is." He marveled at the humorous, sensual goading that came so naturally when he talked to her. "Better still, you come to me. I'm at Burj Al Samaa."

"Your turf is a hotel room?" she finally said. "And what would your terms be? Something from the room-service menu?"

A laugh rumbled from his gut. *Ya Ullah*, but this was new. He'd never enjoyed her wit this much before. But then, he hadn't known she was witty. Now that he thought about it, they'd talked last night more than they'd talked in a month back then. Their limited, stolen times together had been consumed mostly by hot and heavy sex. Back then, all the talking she'd done had been with Jalal. He'd felt left out, and he hadn't even known how much he'd missed.

He wouldn't miss a thing now. He'd have it all. All the fire and friction and fun of her.

"But I'm proposing a continuation of our first round, not a second one. *That* will be on my turf and terms."

"You're…" He could tell she muffled the phone with her hand. He could still decipher what she said. "I'll only be a moment. Sure, I'll take another cup of tea."

His smile froze. She…sounded totally different. Easygoing and eager. She'd never sounded like that with him. Not even when she'd been claiming to love him.

Then he heard the voice that answered her. Distant and muted. But definitely male.

Something hot and harsh spread like an intravenous shot of lava in his veins. Something he'd only ever felt on her account. Jealousy…

Jealousy? Now, *that* was idiotic. There was no application for anything like that in their situation. He shouldn't…*didn't* care what she did or who she did it with.

Even if he was stupid enough to care, she was probably at work, and that was a colleague or an assistant and he was again blowing things out of proportion…

"Listen, you exasperating lout. I spent this morning trying to resolve the mess you left behind, and the only thing I'll do if I come to your temporary turf is kick you where it counts. So it would be potency-preserving for you to get off my case."

Her threats still tickled him. But he couldn't laugh this time. Not after he'd heard her talking to that man. Hearing the difference in her voice now doused his enjoyment.

He still attempted a rejoinder. "Tut-tut, is that any way to talk to your probable new king?"

"First, I'm American if you've forgotten, so at best, the king of Azmahar would be my boss. Second, cows will skate before you become king. So stop wasting everyone's time and fly back to whatever vultures' aerie you swooped down from."

It was no use. Even with the tightness in his chest, which he wouldn't even try to analyze, every word that pelted out of her mouth seemed to find a receptor in his humor centers.

His lips spread. "The only time I'll swoop down will be to carry you away, my luscious lamb."

"Then too late in midair, you'll find out I'm no such thing."

"*Aih.* Thankfully. But the feline you really are is why you found me irresistible."

She used to say he was aptly named, a human lion. He'd called her his wildcat, his lioness, among other things.

"Nowadays, the world doesn't give a fig about your irresistibility, like I don't. But unlike you, who clearly aren't here to take part in resolving the crisis but to indulge in obnoxious score-settling, I have work to do. You had your fun last night, so be a good evil mogul and let me get on with it."

He lay back on the bed, hard as rock again. "How counterproductive can you get? You've just said the magic words that will assure that you won't see the last of me. Not before I make you eat those words, of course. Out of my hand. Again."

She didn't answer for a long moment. His breath shortened, his every muscle quivered with arousal and anticipation. What was that unpredictable storm of fire and femininity up to now?

"Satisfied your last-word syndrome? Just like you did your have-your-way disorder last night?"

And he laughed, deep and delighted. "I knew you had to be brilliant to be where you are today. But that's a truly novel way to have the last word, *ya naari*. I concede. This round goes to you."

"Oh, joy. You mean I can go now?"

"You mean you can't hang up on me?"

She did.

He laughed again, long and loud, as he hadn't done in… probably ever. Certainly never when he'd been alone.

Then he headed to the shower again.

He came out half an hour later, made a few phone calls.

He got the lay of the land, the schedule of relevant events for the next week. The most important function was next evening at the royal palace. A gathering of all political and economic figures engaging in the dance of trying to figure out how not to end up at the bottom of the food chain.

Roxanne was going to mediate the rituals.

Although she'd known because of her sensitive position, he was sure his candidacy wasn't public knowledge yet. Sure, he must have invaded the gossip circles and social media with his stunt at her door by now, but people probably thought he was just passing through, that she was the focus of his visit. He could still resume the secrecy of his purpose in Azmahar.

But she wanted him gone. Better. She'd hurled the gauntlet in his face. That settled it.

To hell with flying under the radar.

Time to prove to her he could get cows to skate.

Time to make an official swoop on Azmahar's vacant court.

The last rays of a blazing sunset were giving way to the dominion of a velvety evening as Haidar arrived at the edifice he'd been recruited to take over.

He pulled his rented Mercedes to a stop in the wide-as-a-four-lane-highway driveway and gazed up at it through the windshield. Twilight conspired with shadow-enhancing, detail-popping lighting to make it look like some colossal creature from a Dungeons & Dragons fantasy.

He exhaled, slammed out of the car. Qusr Al Majd—

literally Palace of Glory—must have seemed like a good idea to Faisal Aal Munsoori, its builder and the founder of Azmahar's now ex–royal family—the regrettable half of his genes. Back in the sixteenth century, overwhelming demonstrations of power, wealth and invulnerability were all the rage, after all.

And though the man's descendants had managed to destroy his legacy, impoverish his kingdom and squander his throne, Al Majd remained one of the world's architectural wonders. Or so it was touted by those who swooned at ostentatious constructions. It certainly gave the overhyped Taj Mahal a run for its money.

But the Taj was doing something useful besides look pretty. He'd certainly have tourists crawling all over *this* place if he ever became king. It should at least earn its keep.

As for him, should the dreaded day come, he'd frequent it only to keep up appearances and conduct power games. But to live, his—as of this morning—house had it beat by light-years.

He handed his keys to a gaping valet, took the hundred and one imperial white granite steps up to the entrance in twos. In moments he was striding through thirty-foot-high, elaborately carved and gilded doors, then crossing the suffocatingly ornate foyer, making a mental note to simplify and modernize the damn place if he ever became its keeper. And to do something about its patrons' sense of style, too.

He swept a coalescing gaze over the loitering crowd, grim humor twisting his lips. Considering that most looked as if they'd stepped out of an Addams-Family-cum-Aladdin masquerade, they had a nerve, gaping at him.

Seemed his presence here really was unexpected. Most probably unwelcome. He might be right, after all, and his recruiters knew nothing about what the people of Azmahar wanted or would accept. That, or the openmouthed gawkers had heard of his escapade at Roxanne's and were trying to imagine him spread-eagle on her bed begging to be used.

Not that either explanation mattered in the least.

He'd taken Roxanne's challenge and would see this game to the end. And if this kingless kingdom needed his leadership, it was damn well getting it.

Without slowing, he headed to his destination. He hadn't been here for over eight years, but he remembered well where all pompous, mostly pointless gatherings took place. In the Qobba ballroom, literally Dome, since it resided under a hundred-foot one at the heart of the palace's main building.

Good thing he also knew the place well enough to have learned its secret shortcuts. He made a set of memorized turns leading to a deserted corridor. Once in its blessed peace and subdued lighting, he breathed in relief to be rid of the bustle and invasive eyes.

Suddenly, footsteps joined his in the muted silence.

They came from behind. Sure, steady. Single. In an alternating rhythm to his footfalls. No attempt to catch up to him, just keeping pace.

A chill crackled through his every nerve.

It wasn't fury that someone was following him. Or even worry at the possibility of an attack.

It was a…presence that had engulfed him.

Immense. Potent. Ominous.

He stopped. So did the steps behind him. He turned slowly, felt the icy menace of that manifestation swirling around, hindering him like a straitjacket of chains. By midturn every instinct was shouting at him, *Don't look back! Just walk away!*

It took all he had to overcome the unreasoning aversion, mostly out of burning curiosity.

Next moment, it was his turn to gape.

Twenty paces away, a man stood so still he might have stopped time in its tracks, so dark he seemed to absorb shadows, snuffing out light. Tall, taller than even him, as broad, in an *abaya* that opened over shirt and pants, falling to the ground like a shroud of night. He projected something far larger than his physical size, emitted a force Haidar had never felt from another human being. His stance was deceptively relaxed, arms passive by his sides, face slightly lowered, dark eyes leveled on him from beneath dense, winged eyebrows, transmitting a message, a knowledge. That it would be at his whim that he walked away from this confrontation. And it looked like…

Rashid?

Every muscle in his body went slack with shock.

But…*no*. It couldn't be. The dimness was playing tricks on his vision, his imagination. He had been thinking of Rashid a lot lately, must be superimposing his memory on this man who resembled him—

"I heard you were pimping yourself out."

A sickening sensation jolted through him. That voice…

It shared elements with the one he'd last heard over the phone. After they'd become enemies. It had been cold and dark then, nothing like the lively, expressive baritone of the man who'd once been his best friend, sometimes closer to him than his own twin. He'd thought the ugly conflict had been coloring it.

It was far worse now. Fathomless with terrible mysteries.

It *was* Rashid. Changed almost beyond recognition, yet undoubtedly him. Then he moved. With every step closer, it became clearer. The orphaned distant cousin who, through what he'd once thought a twist of magnanimous fate, had become the biggest part of his and Jalal's life, had not merely changed.

He'd metamorphosed.

One of the most apparent facets of radical change was his hair. Rashid had always kept it long, to his guardian's distress. It had once reached the middle of his back. Even when he'd joined the army, he hadn't gotten the usual military crop.

It was now almost shaved.

But it was worse than that. As he came to a stop a few feet

away, in the light from a brass sconce, he could see it. A blood-curdling scar slashing its way from the corner of Rashid's left eye down to the corner of his jaw, slithering down his neck, then lower…

"So tell me, Haidar, how long have you been hiding this burning desire to be tied, gagged and abused?"

That new voice, that predatory rumble, revved inside his chest with an oppressive sorrow. For the two-decade friendship that had ended and taken another chunk of his humanity with it.

But regret served no purpose. And his humanity, according to the best of authorities, hadn't existed to start with.

Tilting his head, conceding that there would be no quarter given on either side, his huff was the very sound of bitter amusement. "Dominated. Abused is a whole different sub-category."

"Just goes to show you can never claim to know anyone."

The bile of confusion at how vicious Rashid had become in his enmity rose again. "So true."

Those black-as-an-abyss eyes poured icy goading and burning scorn over him. "Word is you exiled yourself from Zohayd after your mother tried to roast half the region and serve it to you on a platter. I wonder how much effort you put into fabricating that 'fact.'"

Rashid was one of the trio who could ever smash through his defenses, melt the layers of ice at his core. Boil his blood.

But a heated defense was exactly what Rashid wanted.

He'd long been done giving anyone what they wanted from him.

"You know me, Rashid. Such things come to me effort-lessly. I leave it to…lesser men to exert themselves."

Seemingly satisfied he *had* gotten the reaction he'd wanted after all, Rashid said, "So now that Zohayd has wised up and kicked you out on your ear, you've come to blight Azmahar with your presence. But if *you* knew anything about me, you'd know people leave it to me to…deal with discord and its sowers."

Without the tinge of sarcasm in his tone, he would have thought Rashid was deadly serious. Deadly, period. This was the face of someone who would kill without mercy.

As he had before.

Not that it worried him in the least. Two more things he'd been born without were fear and the ability to back down.

He raised Rashid double his provocation. "I just thought I'd come see what I can do to save Azmahar from the dire fate of having to settle for someone with your…fundamental deficiencies. You know how charitable I can be."

Something lethal slithered through the depths of Rashid's eyes—not exactly an emotion, but a reaction. Haidar didn't know why, but it forced his focus back to the scar.

Ya Ullah, how had that happened? When? Not during his army years. He knew that. What he didn't know was why he'd never heard of Rashid having it, or how he'd gotten it. Did anyone know?

He had a feeling no one did. No one but Rashid himself.

"How much did you pay those clans to 'choose' you as their candidate?"

Rashid's voice, harsher now, brought his eyes back to his. He didn't want his scar scrutinized. Especially by him.

Haidar exhaled. "How much did you?"

"I was actually offered whatever I could ask for. A lot of people will do anything to stop you, or your asymmetrical half, from taking the throne."

Suddenly he was fed up. He hated this. Hated that they had to keep stabbing at each other, deepening the wounds, widening the rift. He'd never wanted any of this. Now he wanted it all to stop.

It wouldn't be a concession of defeat if he reached out to

Rashid. It would be an olive branch to an injured adversary. Who should have never become one.

He inhaled. "A throne is something I never thought about or wanted, Rashid."

"That's a famous tactic." Rashid shrugged. "The sour-grapes maneuver. You were the Prince of Two Kingdoms who could never be in line for the throne of, either. What else can you do but pretend you aren't interested?"

"No pretense. After a lifetime of watching what kind of pain in the neck, heart and butt being king is from the woeful example of my father, I wouldn't wish it even on you."

"I'm so touched that you consider me your worst enemy."

Wanting to kick himself for the terribly timed joke, when it was certain Rashid had taken it literally, he started to clarify.

Rashid overrode him. "But don't I now share that status with your pointedly absent semi-demon twin?"

Haidar waited for the mention of Jalal to finish turning the skewer embedded in his gut.

Rashid only stabbed him harder. "I came after you only to tell you how entertaining it will be, watching you two campaign for the throne, adding your arrogance to your uncle's ineptness, your cousins' excesses and your mother's all-round villainy."

Having inflicted all the injuries he'd wanted to, Rashid turned.

He'd walk away, and any chance to heal their severed bond would be lost.

Haidar lunged after him, grabbed his arm.

Rashid's gaze lowered to the fingers digging into his *abaya*-wrapped flesh. Haidar could swear his hand burned.

He didn't care if Rashid possessed heat vision for real and would burn off his hand. He had to know.

"What happened to you, Rashid?"

After a chilling moment, Rashid calmly removed his hand from his arm, stepped away as if Haidar's nearness soiled him.

His gaze was opaque. "You were always a self-involved son of a major bitch, Haidar."

He wasn't up to contesting the accuracy of that summation, wasn't sure how it applied here. "I'm trying to get involved now."

"A bit too late for that. Years too late."

"*B'haggej' jaheem.* Stop being cryptic. How did you get this way?"

"You mean the scar? You should have seen it before the corrective surgery."

Haidar thought his head would burst with frustration. "I mean everything. The visible and…otherwise."

For a long moment it appeared Rashid wouldn't bother answering.

Then he said, "I dropped my guard." His glare could have pulverized a rock. "Trusted the wrong people."

Haidar staggered back a step. "Are you saying I somehow had a hand in this?"

"It's so heartwarming to see how you've mastered self-deception, not to mention self-absolution, Haidar."

Now his brain was threatening to liquefy with incomprehension. "That's insane, Rashid. I know we've had our differences in the past years—"

"You mean we've been trying to destroy each other."

"I've been trying to stop *you* from destroying *me*. And whatever I did in retaliation for your actions, it was only business."

"This…" Rashid tilted his head, giving him an eyeful, slid a lazy finger down the ridge of disfigurement to the base of his neck. Haidar was certain it snaked lower onto his back. It seemed to have forged all the way to the recesses of his soul. "…was only business, too."

Haidar stared at him, helplessness and confusion sinking their claws into his gut. "You're making no sense."

"Neither are you, if you think you can reinstate any personal interaction between us again. And if you think I'd ever be party to making you feel better about yourself in this lifetime, you have me confused with the wrong Rashid Aal Munsoori. One who ceased to exist long ago."

Haidar grabbed his arm again as he started to turn. "Rashid, you at least owe me—"

Rashid rounded on him, snarling. "I don't owe you, or Jalal, or any member of your family a damn thing—"

He stopped, his eyes burning black holes into Haidar's soul.

Then his lips spread in a sinister parody of a smile, his teeth gleaming eerily against his darkened skin.

Haidar barely suppressed a shiver.

What the hell *had* Rashid metamorphosed into?

"I beg your pardon, Haidar." What? "I was inaccurate when I said I don't owe you and your family a thing. I do owe you. A lot of pain and damage. I always pay my debts."

This time when he turned away, Haidar let him go.

Before he exited the corridor, Rashid turned with a serene-as-the-grave glance. "Sit tight, Haidar, and wait for your share of my payback."

Five

I haven't gotten my share of your payback yet?

What were the past two years all about then?

Haidar struggled not to pursue Rashid, tackle him to the ground in front of everyone and force him to explain.

One thing stopped him. Knowing Rashid wouldn't explain, not even if he beat him to a pulp. Not that he could. Not without being pulped back. Which wasn't a bad idea. They could just rip each other to shreds, get the bitterness exorcised and get it over with. Maybe even get back to the way they'd once been.

According to Rashid, that would require a time machine.

But for the present, the opening round was over. Rashid had pulled back to his corner, expecting Haidar to crush his peace offering underfoot as he stomped to his. Instead, he would get informed. He needed knowledge to convince Rashid to call off the fight. Now that he knew Rashid believed he had somehow been party to whatever had happened to him, he would pay any price to learn the truth.

Until then, he had other struggles to handle.

Roxanne. Jalal. Azmahar and its empty throne. Business conflicts with Rashid at their core...*ya Ullah*, Rashid...

He hadn't thought anything could be worse than what had happened with Roxanne. Or Jalal. Or their mother. This was. This won the category of heart-wrenching developments, hands down.

He found himself entering the ballroom. Seemed he'd continued his path on Auto. The expansive space, decked like an Arabian Nights bazaar, only peripherally registered in his awareness.

Then something sharpened his focus. A decrease in the overlapping voices and clinking utensils, the cessation of melancholy Azmaharian music. He zeroed in on the cause.

Roxanne.

She was walking up the stage. Straight, brisk, no shadow of hesitation or self-consciousness, no hint of a sway or curves to distract from her purpose or undermine her efficiency. She was dressed sedately, the flame of her hair subdued in a twist at her nape, her face made up in neutral colors that downplayed her vivacious coloring and the sensuality of her features. How different from the mass of passionate fire he'd lost his mind over eight years ago. Or the bathrobe-decked firebrand he'd done the same with a couple of days ago. This facet of her still aroused the hell out of him.

Seemed she dialed the password to his libido no matter what.

It was incredible for someone of her youth and looks to be taken this seriously in a patriarchal society where chauvinistic tendencies survived to this day. Here it remained accepted that certain roles were male exclusive or dominated, with women like Roxanne being exceptions.

And what an exceptional rarity she was. He luxuriated in her every nuance as she took the podium, addressed the now pin-dropping-silent crowd, cordial, confident, in control. Something thrilled inside his chest. Admiration, pride...

He gritted his teeth. He didn't have to like or appreciate her to give in to his hunger for her. Those sentiments could actually dampen his lust, hamper his plans to satisfy it. This insidious softening had to be curbed. Starting right this second.

He moved out of the shadows. Instead of keeping to the periphery, he cut right through the tables. Might as well get all the staring and exclamations out of the way en masse.

Sure enough, his passage caused a wildfire of buzzing and bustling to sweep through the ballroom.

His progress was unimpeded until he passed by a table populated by his recruiters. Elation replaced their surprise too soon. They pounced on him, eager to show everyone that he was on their coalition's side. He answered them by insisting he was here to perform *independent* research, impatience rising as opposing brands of passion and compulsion burned into him. Rashid's from the entrance, Roxanne's at the podium.

People rushed to make a place for him at the table closest to her, flipping rabid curiosity between them as if watching an unfolding candid-camera show. She waited in seeming calmness for the disturbance to die down and for him to take his seat. But he sensed her fury.

He would have relished it if he wasn't too raw to enjoy more hostility, even one fueled by a hunger as vast as his.

He had to deal with it. Just as she had to with his presence.

She did, glossed over the disruption he'd caused, resumed her opening address before turning over the mic to the first speaker.

He watched her descend the stage, walk to the end of the ballroom. She took a seat aligned with his view of Rashid, who stood alone at the entrance like a demon guarding the mouth of hell. Very symbolic.

He cast each a look, was hurled back a hail of antipathy.

All he needed now was for Jalal to walk in, and the triad of wrath and rejection would be complete.

He exhaled, tried to focus on the proceedings. Though what he hoped to achieve here, he no longer knew.

The people who had mattered most to him hated his guts. He didn't think his transgressions against each warranted that level of acrimony. Seemed just being himself was enough to earn it.

And he thought a whole nation would want him?

Another major point was they—even Rashid with his scars and transformation—were prospering with him gone from their lives.

Maybe that should tell him something. That there was no escaping his mother's legacy. That all he could ever be was a malignant influence. That redemption was out of the question and the best thing he could do for Azmahar was stay the hell away.

He turned one last time to the two who thought that was a given. At the confirmation in their eyes, a conviction took root.

He turned around, giving them his back, one thing settled.

He'd prove them and everyone, starting with himself, wrong.

Three hours of moderating the self-important, conflicting, anachronistically tribal so-called elite would have been enough. But to do it while being subjected to Haidar's burning focus had shot Roxanne's nerves.

She and her team had worked hard to get all major movers and shakers in the kingdom together, find out their positions and see how they'd mix. She was supposed to come out with a firm idea of who could be part of the solution, and who'd better be sidelined.

Then Rashid Aal Munsoori had walked in.

She'd thought the introduction of that superpower this early would disrupt a balance that hadn't yet been found. The man seemed like such a force of...darkness; he'd swayed people just by showing up. And scared them. She'd thought he was the worst thing that could have happened. Then, enter Haidar.

It had been his presence that had polarized reactions, incited passions and generally disturbed everything.

Seemed his effect on people was universally consistent. And *that* when he'd only sat there silently watching.

She'd barely stopped the situation from devolving into a mess.

Avoiding eye contact with anyone, she strode to get out before people could corner her with questions she couldn't or wouldn't satisfy. Before Rashid could cut his way through his detainers to her. Most important, before…

"So the question is—what *was* the point of all that?"

And she'd almost made it!

She just stopped herself from stomping her foot and screeching a chagrined *no*. From running the hell out of there. Right after taking off her high heels and hurling them at Haidar.

Unable to give their audience any indication of how much she'd like his head on a stick, she slowly turned. And almost toppled over.

He'd looked stunning from afar. It was far worse up close. If possible, he looked better than he had two days ago. In a steel-gray suit the exact color of his eyes that worshipped his every inch and flaunted his proportions, he looked like a sun god. Eyes gleaming in the soft-toned ambience, skin glowing like heated copper, hair shimmering like a black panther's coat.

All in all, a divine masterpiece of masculinity. *And* born to exist in backdrops of such opulence, created to justify their extravagance, which showcased his grandeur.

To make it worse, that voice of darkest wine and velvet cascaded over her again. "Was that a drive for the up-for-grabs court? There *are* enough wannabes to turn the strongest stomach."

Her teeth ground together as he left barely enough distance

between them for public decorum, his scent and virility co-cooning her senses, triggering desire and distress.

Somehow she found enough discipline to pretend an impersonal smile for their now-avid audience. "A king doesn't a royal system make. It was agreed that we have to fill the lower slots in the hierarchy before the top is filled."

"So you want the new king to come to a ready-made government. All I can say is, good luck getting Jalal or Rashid to return your calls once you reveal your figurehead intentions."

If she made him think that was what was on offer, it would send him out of Azmahar within the hour.

Too damn bad she was too professional. "It will be a transitional government until a king sits on the throne."

"Then said king will be free to toss whatever pieces he doesn't approve of back in the box?"

"I don't think such unilateral decisions would be welcome anymore in Azmahar."

"You think any of the candidates will even consider such a deficient position? Such limitation of power? Such an upside-down process? You think *I* would?"

"We're just trying to learn from the mistakes of the past."

"Even in democracies, presidents pick their deputies. You expect a king in our region not to pick his trusted people?"

"As long as they are picked through merit, not nepotism."

"That isn't even an issue in my case, or Jalal's or Rashid's, for that matter. We were headhunted because we proved in the big bad world of business and politics that we know who to pick to help us run our multibillion-dollar enterprises. We're not about to become tribal, blood-blinded throwbacks if we sit on a throne."

His eyes were all *gotcha* when she had no ready answer.

Before she could regain ground, he changed direction. "So I understand why my uncle's slew of successors was bypassed for the king's position. Any reason they are now for all other positions?"

That she had an answer for. "For the same reasons you say you understand. Just as the clans' council that formed after the king's abdication refused to let his sons and brothers succeed him, they wouldn't let them assume any significant roles. It was agreed the sons are too inexperienced and the brothers too same-school, and all are guided by the same entourage that damaged Azmahar."

"And you think the bozos present here today are any better?"

"They're here today so we can weed out the bozos."

His lips spread. "It would be far easier to leave those in, and pick out the non-bozo types. Want my advice on how to do it?"

"No. But you're going to blight me with it, anyway."

His grin grew wider. "Play back the evening's taped hoopla. Eliminate anyone who spoke out of turn or lost his temper. You'll be left with five out of five hundred. I counted. Those are the only people *I'd* have in my cabinet."

That was exactly what she'd thought, too. Damn him.

She wasn't about to tell him that. "You're founding a new kingdom and recruiting ministers for it?"

"Cute. But if you don't heed my advice, just have a raffle. Anyone but those five would be equally disastrous, after all."

"Thanks for the gems of wisdom. But we won't do anything until we're in possession of enough data."

"And what else are 'we' going to do?"

"*We* won't do anything. While *I* have to go."

"Good. I'll tag along."

Yeah. Right. She'd sooner have a lion in tow. One just released after a month of captive starvation.

"Why don't you stay and complete the chaos?"

His eyebrows shot up in what must be simulated surprise. "Chaos?"

Her genial expression didn't waver even as her hiss attempted to disembowel him. "I planned this to be a relaxed event, even a bit festive—"

"*That* explains it. I thought you were trying to start a new tradition—Azmaharian Halloween."

She sharpened her tone. "I wanted to put the attendees in the most cooperative frame of mind, to alleviate the mood of doom and gloom that permeates the kingdom. So thanks so much for spoiling everything."

"Me? What did I do?" Those mile-long lashes swept up and down.

She almost felt their swoosh, certainly felt it fan her fire. "You have the superpower of discord sowing. And you have it on constantly, exercise it at will, actively or passively."

She waited for him to volley back something inflammatory and incontrovertible. Lightness only drained, leaving his face bleak.

Then it got worse. Agony flitted through his eyes as they tore away. She followed their trajectory to the most disturbing presence around. Rashid.

As if feeling his gaze, Rashid half turned. And if looks could dismember, Haidar would have been in pieces.

She shuddered at the force that blasted between the two men. Surprisingly, the viciousness felt one-way. What emanated from Haidar was as intense, but different in texture. Something she'd never thought to feel from him. Despondency.

Haidar returned his gaze to her. "Rejoice, Roxanne. I'm taking my disruptive presence away from inhabited areas."

Then he turned and strode out of the ballroom.

Roxanne stared at Haidar's receding back for the second time in as many days. Then she found herself rushing after him.

She had to pour on speed to catch up with him. In a deserted corridor that seemed to materialize out of nowhere.

It was only when she caught him back that her actions sank in.

What the *hell* was she doing?

He turned to her, something like…hurt filling his eyes, and she blurted out, "What's wrong?"

She almost kicked herself. What did she care if anything—if *everything*—was wrong with Haidar Aal Shalaan?

It seemed he wouldn't answer. Then he exhaled. "A lot, evidently. Probably everything."

She should say something borderline civil, get the hell away.

Instead she asked, "So what did I say that triggered your sudden retreat?" At his surprise, she rushed to add, "I'm asking only so I can replicate my success in the future."

She expected him to slam her with something bedeviling. He didn't.

"You…confirmed something Rashid said to me earlier. It wasn't the only time I've noted your corresponding opinions of me."

"We have more in common where you're concerned. I heard you were friends once. Now you're relentless enemies."

She expected him to say *they* weren't enemies, just no longer lovers. A state of affairs he had no problem reinstating.

Again, he thwarted her expectations, nodded, his eyes returning to the deadness, the defeat, that so disturbed her. "I somehow thought our enmity wasn't such common knowledge."

"Are you kidding? Even if my job didn't revolve around keeping track of the honchos of economy, it would have been kinda hard to miss the two most meteorically rising players in the tech world butting heads. You've been giving *Clash of the Titans* a run for its money for the past two years."

"It might be hard for you to believe, but I didn't start it."

"I believe you."

He frowned. "You do?"

"You never 'start' anything. You drive people to the point where they want to take you apart. When they try, you retaliate, viciously, and to the world it seems it's only legitimate for you to do so."

His laugh was bitter. "Of course, *that's* what you believe. And you might even be right. But not in Rashid's case."

"He *is* too powerful for even you to decimate and assimilate."

"I meant I didn't drive him to it. And since you asked, that's what's wrong—being unsure what did. *And* the…conversation we had."

"It shed light on his motivations?"

"More like caused an avalanche that buried them totally."

She hated feeling dismayed on his behalf, glared at him. "It's not possible you don't know."

"I *thought* I knew. That it was another escalating, self-perpetuating train accident of a mess, which the sweeping majority of my relationships have turned into."

Good thing to be reminded of *that* salient point.

He might be unable to connect his actions to the mess he made of people's lives. Didn't make him innocent of the crime.

Hackles rising, she smirked. "Why wonder if it's your M.O.?"

"Because once I saw him again, it ripped me out of the depersonalized war we've been waging on each other and back to the realm of the personal. And none of it made sense anymore."

A knot formed in her throat at his disconsolate tone. "Did you retrace incidents to what could have started this?"

His gaze clouded, as if he had plunged into his memories, before he said, "We were twenty, he was twenty-one." Her chest tightened more when he said *we,* as if he and Jalal were one indivisible unit. "Rashid and I were taking the same courses, already starting up our tech-development projects. Then his guardian died. He hadn't truly needed a guardian beyond early childhood—he'd been earning his own living since his early teens. But his guardian left a mess of debts. And Rashid took it upon himself to repay them. *That* was our first fight.

"I was angry that he'd take on the debts of someone who hadn't taken him in willingly to start with. A man whose sons were living in the luxury their father's debts had provided them with. It was they who should repay that money, not Rashid, whom they'd never treated like family and would have mistreated if not for his closeness to us. But Rashid would sit there and take my anger, and after I exhausted every argument, he would just say the same thing again. His honor demanded it."

"But what did he think he could do? At twenty-one, without a college degree or capital, I can understand he could support himself, but pay off massive debts…?"

He grimaced in remembered exasperation. "He had it all figured out. An American military base was being erected in Azmahar, and the Azmaharian army was having a recruitment drive, promising top recruits incredible financial and educational advancements. He was confident he'd be among those, calculated he'd pay off the debts in five years while doing something he'd always admired and gaining an education he could have never afforded on his own."

"That does sound like a solid plan."

"Not to us. Not to *me*. It was a shock that he'd chosen his university not because it was close to his girlfriend but because it was what he could afford. We were determined to help him, said we'd get the money from our father or older brothers, or make them find a way to get the debts dropped. But the pride-poisoned idiot refused. *He* would honor his guardian at whatever cost."

"I still don't understand why you so objected to his plans."

"Because the cost might have been his *life*."

"Uh…come again?"

"At the time, due to some major stupidities by my uncle and clan, an armed conflict between Azmahar and Damhoor seemed certain. We took turns telling him what a self-destructive fool he'd be to join the army just in time to be sent to war. *Ya Ullah*…how I never throttled him, I'll never know."

Haidar mimed the violent gesture, his whole body bunching, his face contorting with relived frustration and desperation.

It was fascinating, *shattering,* this glimpse into his past. Another reminder that she hadn't known him at all, more proof of how unimportant she'd been that he hadn't shared this with her, clearly a major incident in his life.

But it was worse than that. She'd believed he'd been born without the capacity for emotional involvement. That had mitigated her heartache and humiliation.

But his emotions did exist. And they could be powerful, pure. Seemed it took something profound to unearth them, such as what he'd shared with Rashid. Nothing so trivial as what he'd had with her.

The discovery had the knife that had long stopped turning in her heart stabbing it all over again.

Which was beyond ridiculous. This was ancient history.

What was important here was the history in the making. This was an unrepeatable opportunity to learn vital information about two of the candidates for the throne. It could be crucial to the critical role she was here to play.

Swallowing the stupid personal pain, she forced out the steady words of the negotiator she was. "It sounds like he should have loved you more for caring so much about his well-being and safety."

"Then you don't know much about how young men can be with each other. Our response to fear, for him, of losing him, wasn't pretty. I especially…got carried away." He wiped a palm over his eyes wearily. "We were drawn to Rashid as children when we recognized that he had big problems, too. We had our share, growing up in Zohayd when our non-Zohaydan half belonged to a family everyone despised and a queen everyone hated. But we had a family. Rashid had only us. And we used that. Jalal pressured him through his loyalty to us. But I knew him better, knew pressuring him wouldn't work, knew how to push his buttons. I played as dirty as I thought I had to."

Another reminder what a prince Haidar could be. How he considered any means justifiable to get his end.

"And you failed?" He nodded dejectedly. "So he still left, only with your creative cruelty as his last memory of you."

"Aih." His eyes let her see into a time of personal hell. "Then war broke out. Zohayd and Judar intervened, but not before thousands died on both sides. Rashid was among the missing. We went insane searching for him for weeks. Then he returned, exhausted but unharmed, leading his platoon across the desert."

Wow. Colorful past that Rashid Aal Munsoori had. And undocumented. Beyond basic data, he seemed to have popped fully formed into the business world two years ago.

Haidar went on. "He was decorated a war hero, paid off his guardian's debts, accumulated graduate degrees and promotions at supersonic speed, and took part in two more armed conflicts by the time he was twenty-eight. We were still speaking then."

Which meant it was around the time she'd left Haidar that his breakup with Rashid had also occurred. "So whatever you did before he joined the army wasn't what caused the rift?"

"It caused *a* rift. He'd answer one call out of five, and when he came back on leave, our relationship was never the same. He wasn't. He rarely went out with us, together or one on one, and when he did, he was subdued, weighing every word. It made me so resentful, so damn worried, I think I…" He gave an exasperated wave.

"Overcompensated?" she put in.

His lips twisted in agreement. "Then one day he told me he'd been offered a major promotion, wouldn't say what it was, but that he'd be traveling all the time and off the grid for most of it. I sensed he was telling me not to expect to hear from him again. And again I..."

"Made it sound as if it wouldn't matter to you either way."

"Will you stop retro-predicting what I did?" He drove his hands into his hair, every move loaded with self-recrimination. "But *aih*. Though it didn't happen quite so...peacefully."

She could fill in the spaces with the worst she could imagine.

"He dropped off the face of the earth. Then three years ago, he suddenly called me. He sounded as if he was drunk or high. I was stunned, since the Rashid I knew was a health and sobriety freak. But what did I know about what he'd become in the years since I last saw him? He said he needed help, gave me an address then hung up. I rushed there, found nothing."

"You didn't find him?"

"I found *literally* nothing. No such place existed. I kept calling him, but the number he'd called from was out of range. Days later, he texted me, saying he'd been drinking, and to please forget it. I texted back, begged to see him. He never answered me. Frustrated with his on-off behavior, I did my best to forget it. And him. A year later, right after the mess in Zohayd was resolved, he came back into my life. As enemy number one.

"I thought he was giving me a hard time to get payback, and to prove that he was 'a year older and a light-year better.' So I called him, offered him a partnership, the one we'd dreamed of as boys. He responded that the only and last time he'd put his hand in mine again would be after I'd signed everything I had over to him, and to never contact him again. I was so

OLIVIA GATES   91

frustrated with him and his grudge-holding that I never spoke
to him again. Until today."

He was telling her things she already knew—how he
couldn't see beyond what *he* wanted and felt. He'd done the
same with her. With Jalal. She shouldn't sympathize. But she
did.

Maybe because he was explaining the motives behind his
actions for the first time...? It changed him from a callous
brute to someone who'd never learned how not to appear so.
It painted him in grays instead of blacks.

But it still made no difference to those he'd injured.

He looked at her as if he needed her to tell him he wasn't
crazy. "But none of that explains his enmity, does it? It was
all just...words. And he had to know I didn't mean them."

"So he's a mind reader, too, among his other talents?"

He grimaced. "I mean he *should* have put what I said in
context. Even if he bought every word I said, that still wasn't
a good enough reason to want to bury me alive."

"Depends on what you said."

Admission blared in his eyes. "Unforgivable things."

Another shock to hear him admit that.

"And at first I felt so guilty, I let him tear into me. But
soon his actions made me so mad, I threw myself into what
escalated into a war. I was resigned I was responsible for our
conflict, deserved his enmity and could do nothing but continue our battles. But seeing him in person again today jolted
through me like a thousand volts."

She had to nod. "Quite understandable. He's one scary
dude."

"But that's the problem. That's not the 'dude' I knew. And
that *scar... Ya Ullah.*"

She frowned. "Scar?"

He looked at her as if *she* was crazy. "How can you miss
it? How isn't it common knowledge?"

"I haven't seen him up close. And according to my sources, Rashid's first appearance in Azmahar in the past seven years was today. Seems no one has seen him before to spread the news."

He nodded slowly. "That makes sense."

Not to her. "That's what shook you so much? The change in his appearance?"

"It's not only that. He's become someone totally different."

"Being a soldier can change you. Being in armed conflicts certainly will."

He shook his head. "I thought that, too, but it's more. Something happened to him. Something terrible."

"More terrible than being in a war?"

"Yes. And he believes I had a hand in it."

Her heart kicked her ribs, hard. "Is he right?"

His whole being stiffened, as if she'd kicked him in the gut. "What do you think?"

Haidar was many things. A criminal wasn't one of them. And he would be worse, a monster, if he'd had a hand in his former friend's physical and psychological disfigurement.

She bit her lip. "What will you do to prove him wrong?"

Tension seeped from him—something like…thankfulness?—staining his gaze as he acknowledged her exoneration. "I need to investigate before I can formulate a plan. It'll be harder because I can't have anyone finding out anything I discover when Rashid has gone to such lengths to cover it up."

"Let me know what I can do to help."

This time when his eyes bored into hers, there was no mistaking it. He was grateful. More. Moved.

Tears suddenly stung her eyes. "Haidar…"

Before she could utter another word, she found herself pressed against the wall with two hundred–plus pounds of hard maleness and demand pressing into her every inch. Her gasp of shock was swallowed by his openmouthed possession. His tongue breached her, thrust into her, driving, claiming, conquering.

The taste of him, the heat and feel of him, what he was doing to her, the way his hands sought all her secrets, sparked her ever-simmering insanities. She writhed against him, nothing left inside her but the need for his long-yearned-for assuagement.

He bent, bit her nipples through her blouse, rose to receive her sharp confessions of pleasure. He resumed devouring her as his big, rough hands slid up her thighs, bunching her skirt, pushing beneath her soaked panties, cupping her buttocks with strength and greed, lifting her, spreading her for his domination.

Falling into an abyss of mindlessness, she clung around him, delighting in his bulk and power as he filled the cradle of her thighs, the one thing left to hang on to in her world.

A storm raged through her, rising from the core his hardness thrust and thrust against. Moans spilled from her with his every wrenching kiss as he escalated the rhythm simulating possession into a fever. She opened wider for him, mouth and legs, to do whatever he wanted to her, to give her everything she needed.

"Haidar..."

The coil of tension in her core suddenly snapped. She cried out into his mouth as the pulse of pleasure tore through her. He had no mercy, his every grind against her bucking body continuing to feed it, unwind it, until she was a lax mass of stunned satisfaction in his arms.

He slowed then stopped his thrusts. Then, still hard and pressed against her quivering flesh, his lips relinquishing hers in one last clinging kiss, he raised his head, looked down at her with eyes raging with arousal, heavy with promise.

"I know what you can do to help me, *ya naari*. Let me pleasure you properly, repeatedly, for the rest of the night."

Six

"Come home with me, Roxanne."

Haidar heard his voice, thick, ravenous. Agonized.

His body would implode if she said no now.

But she wouldn't. Every fabulous inch of her voluptuousness was pliant against him with surrender, her eyes stunned with the explosiveness of this encounter, heavy with wanting more.

At least it had been explosive for her. It made him want to thump his chest that he'd made her come, so quickly, so powerfully, without even taking her. It was beyond gratifying to know he could still have her out of her mind with a touch. But his arousal was far past the red zone.

He could have so easily joined her. Her release had almost driven him over the brink. He'd held back with all he had. He would take his pleasure only inside her.

He'd waited too long to have it any other way.

"Say yes, Roxanne." His fingers pressed into the delight of her flesh, his body roaring from the feel of her and the scent of her satisfaction.

Her breasts still shuddered, her chaotic breathing pressing

them against his burning chest. Her full lips, red and swollen
with the savagery of his hunger, trembled. Receding pleasure
and resurging arousal weighed down her lids, ignited her eyes
with an emerald fever.

She would say yes. And he'd spend the rest of the night
possessing and pleasuring her in every corner of the house
he'd bought just for—

Something tugged at the edge of his clouded awareness. A
sound. The unhurried, powerful rhythm of footsteps…

She stiffened. Then she exploded, pushing him away as if
she'd found herself wrapped around a slimy monster.

Unable to think, to move, he stood frozen as she struggled
to pull down her skirt. Then, without looking back, she ran
away.

"I am really curious, Haidar."

Rashid.

He turned, his body clamped in a vise of agony.

Rashid was approaching from the direction of the ballroom
this time, his progress slow, steady, his face impassive. Haidar
answered his empty stare with a glare reflecting the storm that
still raged inside him. Rashid would no doubt add to the havoc.

"Tell me, Haidar, how did you manage to reach any level of
success, let alone your admittedly impressive one? Men who
can't keep it in their pants aren't known for the discipline and
acumen needed to attain, let alone maintain, success."

Haidar gritted his teeth against the urge to blacken Rashid's
darker-than-sin eyes even more. "After payback already,
Rashid?"

"Actually, I'm doing you a favor. A juvenile demonstration at the door of the kingdom's foremost politico-economic
consultant is one thing. Especially since reports confirm you
stayed at her place only long enough to get your face slapped.
And she made the rounds next day like a mother apologizing
for her delinquent teenager's antics. But to…sexually harass

her in the middle of a public and vital function she organized, in a corridor, against a wall? I really had to break that up."

"And you're calling this a favor…how? Saving my image? Aren't you supposed to be pulverizing it?"

The scorn in Rashid's eyes could have frozen him, if he wasn't seething. "I'm not using the handicap of your sexual adolescence to beat you, Haidar. Not when there is such an array of far more relevant vices to discredit you with."

"Best of luck with that, Rashid. And just so we're clear, with the way your…favor might have crippled me for life, I think I now hate you as much as you evidently hate me."

"Then my work is done. For today." Rashid gave him a mock bow, slowed down a fraction as he passed him. "And Haidar, this woman—she's good."

Blood shot in his head as he grabbed Rashid's arm. "Don't you ever *dare*—"

Rashid cut his rising fury short, serenely removing his hand. "She is *very* good. I watched her tonight, watched others as they responded to her, questioned them extensively afterward. She's putting together what looks like Azmahar's only chance for stability until our little pissing contest is concluded. Don't sabotage her credibility and effectiveness."

With that, he continued on his way, his *abaya* and that aura of inhumanity billowing around him like a malevolent force field.

He didn't look back.

Haidar was getting used to everyone doing that.

But he had to concede that Rashid was right about one thing.

He was in danger of destroying everything he'd ever achieved. He'd been making uncharacteristic mistakes for the past two years. He'd managed to rectify each so far. But his inability to predict consequences had been coming faster since he'd returned here. Since he'd seen Roxanne again.

He'd come here thinking he'd fulfill his objectives. Nudge Roxanne toward the bed he had prepared for her, and perform a preliminary feasibility study of his candidacy.

But not only had he crashed headfirst into Rashid's unexpected reappearance and uberhostility and disrupted the proceedings he'd intended to learn from, he'd ended up pouring out his bewilderment to Roxanne before losing control and nearly consuming her whole. Against a *wall*.

So, a roundup of the evening? Rashid had had the first and last word. Roxanne had eluded him again. He'd learned zip. And his mind and manhood had been dealt near-crippling blows.

Not waiting for the pain to subside, since it probably wouldn't tonight, he exited the corridor of chaos. He plowed through the masses of people who now tried to swarm him, and for the first time since he'd come to Azmahar, wished his bodyguards were around. He'd ordered Khaleel to keep them away, to Khaleel's anxious chagrin, not wanting them around to witness his encounters with Roxanne. Without them running interference for him, it took him longer to extricate himself from the throngs. It was an endless ten minutes before he was on his way back to his hotel.

He couldn't go to his new house. His fantasies of continuing the night there with Roxanne were so vivid, they might cause him permanent damage if he went alone.

But…maybe he didn't have to go alone.

Fully hard again with anticipation, he dialed her number.

His call was rejected. By the third time, he got the message. The insanity had lifted and her unclouded mind was screaming at her—and probably at him—in outrage for what the gross indiscretion he'd dragged her into might have cost her. She might even think it *had* cost her everything. She hadn't looked back, hadn't seen who'd walked in on them.

He parked in the first off-road shoulder, texted her. It was only Rashid.

It was after he'd resumed driving that it hit him.

Only Rashid? What was wrong with him?

She must now be going ballistic, thinking she'd exposed herself as terminally ditzy and in *his* power to the man whose opinion mattered more than the rest of the kingdom combined.

Swearing at himself, he parked again, texted again. It's purely on me in Rashid's opinion. He thinks you're good. Very good. His words. Absolutely no harm done.

Hoping this was enough to alleviate her anxiety, he resumed his drive. He would give her time to go home, then show up at her door.

No, he couldn't. He never repeated himself.

He needed a new strategy. He'd been going about his pursuit all wrong. He'd been too impatient, too hungry, hadn't been listening to her properly. He now realized the only reason she'd been resisting him was her dread of compromising her position.

In the past, she'd initially held him off to protect her mother's and her own reputation in Azmahar's conservative society. He'd gone to great lengths to arrange for their relationship to remain a secret to free her from that fear. Of course, that had served his purposes, too.

But she was now more serious than ever about her image. So if he stopped his impulsive incursions, assured her of privacy and secrecy, he'd bet she'd beat him to that bed. Just as she had in those months of stolen passion.

Rashid, damn it, had been right about this, too. He couldn't compromise her. For every reason there was.

He needed to locate some restraint. And he'd thought he had nothing but. Seemed that was only because there'd been no temptations.

But seeing this matured Roxanne, discovering this new ability to talk to her, the even more intense sexual affinity... now, *that* was temptation.

It was merciful he posed as overwhelming a temptation to her.

Now to make it safe for her to give in to it, to him, fully.

Absolutely no harm done.

Roxanne stared at Haidar's text message for what must have been the thousandth time in the past week.

There'd been dozens more since. But this was the one she kept scrolling back to. And every time she read it, she wished he were in front of her. So she could break his jaw.

She'd been burning with mortification since that day. She'd seriously considered running out of the royal palace and out of Azmahar. She'd been certain her job had been ruined, that she'd be the laughingstock of the kingdom within hours. Maybe the world, if her viral video prediction to Haidar came to pass.

Haidar had played her like the merciless pro that he was. Softening her with one unexpected reaction after another before slamming her with that sob story, the glimpse into the vulnerability she hadn't believed existed. As his coup de grâce, he'd trained stirred and shaken eyes on her, and she'd melted in his arms. Literally. Anyone could have walked in on them and seen her wrapped around him and in the throes of orgasm.

Rashid Aal Munsoori had.

And Haidar had *dared* to say absolutely no harm done!

It didn't matter that he *had* been trying to reassure her that the incident wouldn't cost her her reputation and position. It didn't matter that she had seen Rashid twice since then, and he'd treated her with utmost respect and decorum, without a trace of knowing in his eyes. It didn't matter that there *did* seem to be no harm done whatsoever.

She still wanted to do Haidar some serious harm.

He'd probably encourage her to. And love every second.

Well, she'd get the chance to oblige him in an hour's time.

She was heading to his house. His turf. And on his terms.

He had managed to make it an official summons, too.

But at least she was one of many. A whole delegation had been summoned to said turf to discuss what she regretfully admitted were relevant and pressing matters.

He *had* been laying much-needed groundwork in the past week, dealing with so much. And to her surprise, he was working, if indirectly, with both Rashid and Jalal to manage the oil spill. The three of them, each with his specific powers and strategies, and with their considerable connections, had surrounded the problem from all sides and were well on the way to resolving it.

She'd joked to her team this morning that the plan to save Azmahar should have three kings playing musical thrones.

He'd summoned the five men that he referred to as his "cabinet" to discuss some of the other serious economic and diplomatic problems. She was to act as analytical statistician of the meeting with Sheikh Al-Qadi. Her job, really.

Not that that made her feel any less…violent toward Haidar. In fact, it inflamed her more that he was having her walk into his lair under a pretext to which she could have no valid objection.

She exhaled, cursed the heavy, liquid throb of arousal that was her perpetual state now. That he managed to keep her in it by remote control was the height of injustice.

Why couldn't she feel this way about someone…human?

Resigned that he had her hormonal number, she turned her eyes to the scenery rushing by the window of the limo he'd insisted on sending her.

Suddenly, the terrain changed, from flat desert to a stunning system of dunes that undulated down to an incredible stretch of red-gold shore. It curved into a bay ending in an arm of land that almost touched an oasis of an island. Between the dunes and the shore lay an estate spread with palm and olive trees. Nestled in its heart was a house.

As the car descended on a winding path from the main road, the house came into clearer and clearer detail. It was… amazing. As pliant as a tent that would billow in the warm, dry winds. As fluid as a ship that would sail down the pier that extended from its enfolding terrace, sail away into the sea. It lay like a graceful hybrid among the sublimely landscaped and the divinely natural, adorned with a mile of emerald and aquamarine liquid.

She sat up, heart hammering, mouth drying.

The sheer beauty of it all, enhanced by the perfection of a golden sunset, soaked into her senses, wrenched at every one with a power that left her gasping with its force, its…futility.

So this was Haidar's home in Azmahar. A home he'd one day share with the woman he'd choose. The family he'd make.

This was also the home he'd asked her to come to last week. In her case, "home" had been only a figure of speech.

She'd always known that. Even when she'd been deluded that he'd felt something genuine for her, *Haidar* and *home* had been two words she'd known would never belong together.

They'd always met on impersonal ground, arrived separately, left the same way. How ironic was it that this time, he'd invited her to a personal place for impersonal business?

She blinked back the pointless disappointments as the car passed through electronic, twenty-foot, wrought-iron gates, wound up a cobblestone driveway and approached the architectural work of art from the back. The grounds were so extensive that it took almost ten minutes to come to a stop by the thirty-foot-wide stone steps that led to the entrance patio.

She thanked the driver, got out of the car before he could open the door for her, stiffened her back and resolve as she climbed the stairs. She wasn't waiting for anyone, starting with Haidar, to receive her or wait on her. She was here for business, would conclude it and leave.

She tried not to notice more about the place. She might have achieved that—had she been carried in unconscious. As it was, she absorbed every detail as she reached a wrap-around terrace from which every aspect of the magnificent property could be seen.

The double doors of the house were open. No one was around. Seemed Haidar still didn't believe in having people around.

She stepped into the house, and air squeezed out of her lungs.

Like the exterior, the interior married the unexpected in a seamless blend, old Arabia concepts with innovative themes, producing something unprecedented. Everything had been chosen with an eye for the comfort of both body and soul, blending sweeping lines and spaces with bold wall colors and honey-colored ceilings. Curved windows and doorways coalesced with sand-colored marble floors accentuated by vivid mosaic. Furniture both functional and artistic offset wide-open seascapes. A place of contrasts, from the sublimely relaxing to the vibrant and exotic, an oasis of the best nature and man had been able to produce.

And that was just what she could see of the foyer and sitting area. She didn't want to know what...other rooms looked like.

"I named this placed Al Saherah."

His voice hit her dead center in her heart.

Al Saherah. The Bewitching. The Sorceress.

She turned, found him filling an archway leading to another part of the house. All in white, a fallen angel masquerading as one of the good guys. Big, vital, painfully beautiful.

It was he who was *saher.*

She swallowed the ache the sight of him always struck in her heart. "This place *is* magical."

He walked toward her, as majestic and potentially lethal as the feline he'd been named for. "But I'm thinking of adjusting the name to Al Naar Al Saherah. Or Al Saherah Al Nareyah. To describe its flesh-and-blood personification."

Bewitching Fire. Or the Fiery Sorceress.

Her hand rose involuntarily to her hair. When had he learned to talk like that? Wasn't it enough that he drove anyone with double-X chromosomes insane with lust just by existing? He'd picked up the deadly power of verbal seduction, too? Talk about overkill.

Declining to comment on this salvo of mind-messing flirtation, she cleared her throat. "So where is everyone convened?"

"We met in this awesome inside garden that has the most amazing aqueduct system running through it. Let me show you." He grabbed her hand, tugged her behind him, his grin gleeful like a boy unable to wait to show off a discovery.

She hurried to keep up with him, blinking at his enthusiasm, at the adjectives and intensifiers.

Strange. She'd thought he was too jaded to appreciate material beauty. Or at least that he would be so used to this place, he wouldn't even see its wonders anymore.

As they passed another sitting area, he turned to her. "I fell for this place at first sight."

So. He fell for places. Felt for friends. That made sense. After all, this place *was* unique. And Rashid certainly was one of a kind. But when it came to women, Haidar was indifferent. She'd bet the only reason he wanted her now was the challenge she represented.

She'd better not stimulate his feline tendencies anymore. If she played dead, he'd get bored and go chase some other prey. But—

She stopped so suddenly that she wrenched her hand from the glove of his. He turned to her, eyes questioning.

"You said you *met*." Incomprehension rose in his eyes. She

whacked his arm as hard as she could. "They're no longer here, are they?" His admission was a nonchalant shrug. She hit him harder, her hand stinging from the force of the smack. "You tricked me!"

He rubbed his arm, his eyes flaring, his lips filling. "I didn't. You insisted on coming late."

"There was no need for me to attend lunch, and I wanted you to have time alone with the others. My presence would have only been needed while you wrapped up the meeting."

"And we had to conclude it earlier than expected. Businessmen don't have their time under control. They had to leave."

"You could have told me not to bother coming."

"But I wanted you to come."

His voice, his eyes as he said that…

Images exploded in her mind, sensations in her body. Of every time he'd demanded she come for him, of the last time she had…

She pressed her head between her fists, trying to stop the surge of madness, fury and frustration almost as fierce. "I get that no one walks out on you. Hell, no one is allowed free will around you, and you want to punish me for both transgressions. You headed to my place fresh off the plane with that in mind. So what will it take to satisfy you? Is ruining my career a must?"

"That's the last thing I want, Roxanne."

She staggered back two steps for the one he took closer. "Excuse me as I believe the proof of your actions instead."

His gaze became serious, soothing. "Whatever I did that compromised you, or could have, I didn't plan any of it."

She huffed incredulously. "I wonder how that would hold up in front of a judge. 'I didn't plan to run the lady over, Your Honor.'"

His lips twisted. "*Zain*. I deserve that. And I have no defense. Premeditation isn't better than negligence from the victim's point of view. But I swear to you, I never meant you harm. And I will never compromise you again."

She stared at him. "You mean you'll leave me alone?"

"I mean I'll be the essence of discretion as I do no such thing." He reached for her as he spoke.

This time, she didn't move away. This train *would* hit her. Why pretend outrunning it was an option?

"Roxanne…" He groaned as he enfolded her into his large body.

As if feeling her surrender, he crushed her to his hardness, making no attempt to temper the carnality of his response, of his intentions.

He wanted sex. Raw and raunchy. Dominant and devastating. No pretense of gentleness or emotion. He'd exploit her body and take his pleasure in every way he pleased, plumb her flesh for all the ecstasy she could withstand.

She wanted all that. She was disintegrating with needing it.

She pushed out of his arms.

It took all of Haidar's restraint not to yank Roxanne back and down on any horizontal surface and caress her until he'd aroused her out of resistance.

Not that her reticence was physical. Her arousal cloaked him in echoes of their pleasure-drenched nights, slashed him down to the beast at his core. It had him an inch away from devouring her, riding her hard, shattering her with pleasure, so she'd never again contest his ownership of her flesh, of her every response.

"Roxanne…"

Her raised hand stopped him. What was she…?

Then both hands rose up to her hair, took the pins out. It cascaded in waves of flames down to her shoulders.

Before another neuron could fire a thought, a response in his brain, she was pushing her jacket off her shoulders, then unbuttoning her blouse, revealing the creamy globes of her breasts. *Ya Ullah*, she was…was…

She was stripping for him.

His lungs burned. His hardness passed the point of pain.

He heard himself choking on "While this might be a delight after I've taken you ten times or so, right now it's agony not being the one undressing you."

He reached for her again, expecting her to sweep him away, to continue punishing him with her striptease torture. Again she did something that shocked him into another detonation of arousal.

She grabbed him, climbed onto him, wrapped her legs around his buttocks, digging her high heels into his flesh as she bunched her hands in his hair and brought his lips crashing down on hers.

"Roxanne." His growl was that of a predator at the end of his tether. She pushed against him, making him stagger back and sit down on a couch with her on top. Before he could drag in another breath, she was tearing open his shirt, sinking her teeth into his chest and sucking his flesh.

He bucked beneath her, the pleasure of each nip and suckle acute distress. "Roxanne, let me…"

She slipped from his hold, ended up on her knees between his splayed thighs, her hands as feverish as her lips on the buttons of his jeans.

He watched her, his brain, every inch of him overheating from the sight of her beautiful hands dragging down his pants, dipping into his briefs to greedily surround his erection.

His mind hazed, his body hurtled beyond his control with the first touch of her lips on the oversensitized head.

How he'd missed her touch, her mouth, her breath on him. How he'd hungered for her answering hunger, for her delight in him, in all the liberties he gave her with his body.

But this was spiraling out of control. He had to…needed to slow down, savor it, stop her…

Her hot, moist mouth engulfed almost half of him, the tip hitting the back of her throat.

"Ya Ullah, kaif betsawwi hada?" he raved, mindless now, his hands frenzied in her silken hair. "How do you do that? Make every touch ecstasy?"

She gazed up at him, let him see how she took him, loved it, how her lips and hands milked his hardness. A hot tide surged upward from his loins, outward to his every skin cell. His buttocks and thighs tightened with holding it back. He pulled at her, needing to have this completion within her, *with* her.

She moaned her refusal to let go, the vibration an electro-cuting surge of stimulation from every inch she devoured to his every nerve ending.

He collapsed back, surrendered to her demand, liquid fire flooding from the depths of his loins. He froze in the intensity of the moment, trapped in the excruciating pleasure that had him on the verge of splintering into a million pieces.

Just before he exploded, he tried to wrench himself out. She held on, her lips and hands making insistent sweeps, inciting him to madness. And he lost the struggle.

He shouted her name, threw his head back, dug his hands in the depths of her silk fire and spilled his seed on her tongue.

She held his eyes as he bucked again and again into her hold, as she drained him to the last drop.

A long, long moment passed before she let him slip from her reddened, swollen lips. He lay there, gulping air, staring into the depths of her magical eyes and instead of satisfac-tion, passion roared again, consuming his body in a fiercer fire. Hers. She'd always been what ignited him. What satis-fied him.

He tried to pull her up, bring her over him. She pushed his

hands away. Before he could move, she stood up, her eyes smoldering down at him, her voice husky.

"I owed you one. Now we're even."

Then she turned and walked away.

Seven

Haidar's paralysis lasted only seconds. Then he was on his feet, shoving himself back into his pants and bounding after her.

She was buttoning her blouse as she strode away, then finger-combing her tousled hair. He knew she heard him coming. She clearly had no intention of stopping, or letting him stop her.

He did. By taking away her means of walking.

He swept her off her feet, smiled down at her. "Though that was almost literally mind-blowing, who says we're even? You owe me eight years' worth of pleasure."

"Eight minutes' worth is all you get from this gal. Now put me down before I give your perfect nose some crooked character."

He gathered her hands in one of his. "You have to regain the use of your hands first."

He strode to the bedroom suite he'd picked as theirs, expected her to struggle, make good on her threat. She just looked up at him, her normally communicative eyes empty of expression.

How he wanted her. The pleasure she'd just given him had only intensified his need for her. His need to pleasure her in return was also reaching critical levels. He wanted her naked and hot and writhing beneath his hands, his lips, bucking under his body, convulsing around him, her release wrenching his from his depths.

He reached the bed he'd bought just for her, huge and firm and covered in sheets a darker shade of her eyes. He hadn't thought she'd be here this soon. Someone out there must believe he deserved something fantastic for a change.

Laying her down, he descended on top of her, groaning at the feel of her cushioning him, the only flesh he'd ever felt a part of his own. His lips sought hers. She turned her face away.

He trailed his lips down her face, neck, down to the swell of her breasts. "Do you know how many nights I lay awake, craving to feel you like this? Hearing your moans, your sighs and cries, the memory of your body enfolding mine echoing in my cells until I felt they'd burst?"

Her answer was tight-lipped. "How many? Two?"

A spasm twisted inside his chest. "More like two thousand."

"And did you feel that way on those nights, before or after you had sex with another woman? Or three?"

He rose on both arms, frowned down at her. "We're not going there. What we did or didn't do in the past eight years isn't relevant. We're going to enjoy each other now, as we are today." His lips spread again at the sight of her beneath him, ripe and trying not to arch into him. "And from today onward, I am all for any kind of game you want to indulge in."

She pushed at him. "The only game I want to try is hide-and-seek, where you hide, and I don't seek you ever again."

His frown returned. "You're...angry?"

Her eyes spat emerald daggers at him. "Give the man a medal."

"I thought it was part of this sensual game you started. You were always all for those, too."

"Are you high on something? Like insensitivity and arrogance?"

He rolled to his side and watched in confusion as she scrambled away from him. "But I apologized and promised our liaison will never compromise you again."

She rounded on him as she rose from the bed. "And as a first step in assuring this, you had your driver leave me with you in an empty house. The news will be all over Azmahar by now."

"I flew Haleem in from Zohayd. He's fully Zohaydan and wouldn't reveal anything about you at gunpoint. It's why I insisted you come alone. I told my visitors I had informed you they had to leave, so you 'wouldn't bother coming.'"

She tore her gaze away, looked around the spacious room as if noticing it for the first time. He tensed as he waited for her reaction. He'd spent most of last week preparing it.

It was he who felt rewarded. A wave of pleasure washed over him as she stood bathed in the gold-tinged lights he'd carefully installed to showcase her, framed by the color scheme of fire and emerald he'd meant to reflect hers. Gauzy curtains billowed at the balcony doors behind her like swirls of magic, and her hair stirred in the evening sea breeze like tongues of dark flame.

His fiery goddess in all her glory. At least, in her still exasperatingly clothed one. Soon he'd have all that voluptuousness displayed for his pleasure, his worship.

Thankfully, the sensual ambience he'd tailored for her had an as-clear effect on her.

She was more flushed, less steady as she turned to him. "You put a lot of thought and effort into this, didn't you?"

If only she knew how much. Even he was still smarting from parting with that much cash. "Anything to help you relinquish your worries and inhibitions. And after what you just did to me while still suffering from both, I don't know if I'll survive when you let them go completely."

Her face hardened. "This new discretion is for yourself."

He exhaled, perplexed by her continued resistance. "It *is* also for me, since I get to have you. But—"

She cut him off. "You recognized you were being a self-defeating idiot. I bet it took seeing Rashid to make you realize that, and that the throne isn't in your pocket no matter what scandals you cause. You have to clean up your act if you're to have a prayer against him. Now you'll play the committed, conservative contender and shove me back into the dirty-secret slot."

He found himself on his feet, facing her across the bed, memories unraveling with a sick charge along his every nerve.

"What's this? Anyone would think it's you who have a grievance against me, that I'm the one who walked out on you. May I remind you that you are the one who left when I outraged your sense of independence, sinned in believing I was more than an 'exotic fling' to you? And are you pretending that keeping our relationship secret wasn't exactly what you wanted, then and now? I'm giving you what you always wanted. No demands on my side, no obligations on yours, only no-consequences indulgence. What more do you want?"

Why? How?

She'd long known that he felt nothing for her. So why and how did getting confirmation of that tear her apart all over again?

He came around the bed, raven hair raining down his forehead, the shirt she'd torn hanging open to reveal the magnificent sculpture of his torso, which she'd barely had a chance to worship.

He stopped less than a foot away, bearing down on her with

his overwhelming beauty and rising exasperation. "What kind of game are you playing now? What's with the indignant act? According to you, we had only a sexual liaison, and you ended it. Now that it would be feasible and pleasurable for both of us to resurrect it, why are you behaving as if I once betrayed you? As if I'm degrading you and trying to take advantage of you?"

"Because you did. And you are."

He stared at her as if she'd grown a third eye.

And everything she'd spent years holding back came flooding out.

"Being honest about how you'll take what you want and give nothing in return doesn't make you honorable. And it sure as hell doesn't make you the wronged party here. It only makes you an unfeeling bastard who cares only about getting what you want, who would use anyone in the most horrible way for your own purposes, even the trivial one of telling someone 'I told you so.'"

Every word fell on him with the visible effect of a slap. "*B'haggej' jaheem*, what the *hell* are you talking about?"

And she shouted, *"I'm talking about your bet."*

He stumbled back, his face going slack with shock, reactions rioting across his eyes.

Then he finally rasped, "You know."

It was a statement. An admission. At last.

She'd thought it would bring her relief. It didn't.

Feeling hers eyes tearing, she tore her gaze away, looked feverishly around for her sandals.

She shoved her feet into them, tried to regain her shaky balance. "Thank you for not insulting me more by pretending you don't know what I'm talking about."

"You heard me and Jalal that night."

The same conclusion Jalal had come to. She hadn't refined his deduction.

She did Haidar's. "That was only how I made sure."

He blocked her path as she tried to head for the door. "How did you find out in the first place?"

"I don't owe you anything, least of all an explanation. And if you want someone to play sexual games with, I can recommend dozens for you to pick from. I'm sure you have your own waiting list."

He spread his arms, stopping her from circumventing him, his face gripped in urgency and frustration. "*B'Ellahi,* Roxanne, just tell me!"

Her chest heaved with the remembered humiliation, her eyes threatening to pour long-dried tears. "How do you think?"

Realization detonated in his eyes. Certainty. He dropped his arms, staggered away. "My mother."

She let the entrenched fury in her eyes confirm.

"How did *she* know?" he groaned.

She shrugged. "She said she knows everything about you and Jalal. But especially you."

Agitation receded in his eyes, determination filtering into its place. "I need to know everything she said."

"I'll tell you what *my* mother said. When you approached me at that ball expecting me to fall at your feet."

Heated recollection overlapped agitation in his eyes. "Your words were cool but your eyes were incendiary. I could think of nothing but erasing your reluctance, making you admit that your desire was as instant and as powerful as mine."

She backed away as if from the memories. "The jury will remain out on *that* similarity. But my mother saw you for what you are. She also saw that you had me blinded and realized that to stop me from falling for your seduction, she had to tell me a secret."

"What secret could she have told you? I have none."

"Of course you don't. You keep your vices and transgressions proudly out in the open."

That silenced him. His steel eyes, so like his mother's, turned black. As if her opinion hurt.

She ignored the spasm of guilt at what she had to admit was a gross exaggeration. "It was a secret of hers. During her first stint in Azmahar. She was beginning her career, and she fell madly in love with a royal. She discovered his illegal activities, yet still couldn't walk away. But he fabricated evidence against her, preempting her in case she attempted to expose him, forcing her to leave the kingdom in silence or she would have been publicly disgraced and prosecuted."

His eyes narrowed. "Was that man your father?"

It was the first time he had asked her about her parentage. "No. My father was a one-night stand she had when she returned home from Azmahar heartbroken. But years later, that royal found himself in need of her support and got her an even better post in Azmahar. She was in no position to say no. That was when we came here. He tried to weasel himself back into her good opinion and bed, but she told him where he could put his lies and platitudes."

He said nothing, waiting for the punch line.

She delivered it. "Moral of the story—don't get involved with a royal. He will use you for his whims and abuse you for his benefit. And when I didn't listen, worse happened to me."

His frown turned spectacular. "What do you mean, worse?"

"You didn't even notice that my life was being messed up and my future destroyed. The one thing that mattered to you was that I showed up for your scheduled sex sessions."

"Are you talking about the setbacks you had in your studies?"

Her heart lurched. "So you knew. And you didn't ask me about it, or even offer a word of concern or encouragement."

His already black frown darkened. "Jalal informed me you'd started out so far at the top of your class, you were in one of your own. He made it sound as if I was the reason you were falling behind. I...didn't know what to say. Or do."

"You thought our liaison and the hoops you made me jump through to maintain its secrecy were taking their toll on me, but tough for me, right? You had your pleasure and your convenience, and to hell with me and my future."

He grimaced again. "All I saw at the time was that you'd told Jalal, but not me."

"And we're back to the one thing that matters to you. Your rivalry with Jalal."

"It wasn't like that. This was about you."

"Sure. It was so about me you didn't care that my academic progress was in jeopardy, even when you believed you were the reason for the deterioration. You knew me so little you believed I'd let an affair stop me from excelling in my work."

"But...if I wasn't the reason, then..." He stopped, shock blossoming in his gaze all over again.

"And he sees the light. Yep, your mother again. She had more influence in Azmahar than the rest of the royal family put together. Your efforts at secrecy worked on my mother and the rest of the kingdom, but your mother knew everything about us and decided to rectify the situation. I found out how when I was protesting my inexplicable grades to my favorite professor. She confessed she and the rest of the staff had instructions to increase pressure until I had to leave to save what I could of my future. She said I would harm her if I didn't keep it a secret and advised me to stop whatever I was doing to be on your mother's bad side. *You* were the only thing I was...doing."

"And you never told me."

"I didn't know if I could. You always seemed to be...hers." His face became stone, his eyes flint. She didn't care if that affronted him. It was the truth. "But I *was* guilty of romanticizing you, believing I mattered to you, against all proof to the contrary. I ended up deciding to tell you, thought you might intervene, stop her from destroying my education. Uncanny woman that she is, she seemed to smell my intention and preempted me. She had me brought to her. It was quite an eye-opener, meeting her in the flesh. I understood so much about you, then.

"She prefaced her venom by saying she'd tried to be merciful, tried to let me leave with my pride intact. But since I was so foolish as to invite a confrontation, she had to destroy it. She informed me of your bet with Jalal. She was very proud of your talent for manipulation, which you inherited from her and honed with your rivalry with Jalal. I might not have seen it that way then, but I do now. I owe her a ton of gratitude."

His nonexpression, which she'd once thought indicated he felt nothing, cracked, and bewilderment flooded in.

She explained. "Though she was—and no doubt still is—a vile snob, it was her wish to get rid of me sooner rather than later that stopped me from being the unwitting pawn in your power games with Jalal any longer. She read my disbelief, told me to go demand the truth from your own mouth.

"Before I could, you called me and ordered me to drop everything and go to you. I was stupid enough to hope you'd say it wasn't true, or at least have some excuse to mitigate the sheer petty evil of it all. I was so anxious to clear everything up, I arrived at the apartment before you did."

His eyes closed for a moment, opened. "You were there all along. You heard everything Jalal and I said."

Hot needles pushed behind her eyes. "It was only then that I realized the depth of your resemblance to her. And I decided I wouldn't give either of you that last triumph over me. You wouldn't see me humiliated and heartbroken, and she wouldn't see me running off with my tail between my legs. Your mother raised you to use everyone in your power games—mine raised me to never relinquish equal ground."

Time stretched after she'd said her last word.

It seemed an eternity later when he finally spoke. "So everything you said, every word that has been echoing in my mind ever since, was just you maintaining said equal ground."

Her nod was terse. She was giving him validation in retrospect. Any denigrating thing she'd said had just been a desperate attempt to walk out of that battlefield in one piece.

She didn't care. Let him have his triumph.

"What about the things you said before that day, Roxanne?"

He wanted more. A full admission. He might as well have it.

"That I loved you? I meant it, wholeheartedly." She looked away, unable to bear the terrible loss mushrooming inside her all over again. "Not that I ever blamed you for that. You made it clear you had nothing to give me, were true to yourself, to your principles. As you pointed out the first night you came back, love isn't something your species values or tolerates. If I was stupid enough to give it to you, it was unasked for, unwanted, and I had no right to complain when my heart was trodden on."

Another heart-shredding moment of silence passed.

Then he whispered, "I didn't initiate that bet, Roxanne."

"I know. Jalal told me he did."

He stiffened.

Of course. Jalal. The one thing sure to provoke a profound reaction in him. "Don't tell me you forgot about it in minutes, too."

Tension deflated out of him on a heavy exhalation. "I won't tell you that. I can't. I never forgot the bet."

Was there no limit to the hurt this man could inflict on her?

She let out a choppy breath. "Thanks for not wasting either of our time on insincerities."

Something bruised filled his eyes. "I remembered it constantly because I was jealous. Of Jalal. He was coming close to you in ways I was unable to. I didn't know how to get you to talk to me, laugh with me as he did. All I had was your physical hunger. So I took all I could of it, aroused it as fiercely and frequently as I could, hoping it would be enough. It never was."

She hadn't expected him to bother explaining. She didn't want him to explain. She'd long been resigned that she knew all the answers. She didn't want him to threaten that security.

Before she could tell him to let the past lie in its grave, he went on. "At one of the functions you attended with your mother, where you avoided me per our agreement, you were so…at ease with Jalal. You both seemed so delighted with each other. And my mother—*ya Ullah*, my mother again—she commented on how much you had in common. My unease started to turn to dread then." Her heart scrambled its rhythm, her eyes burning as he held them in a vise of bleakness. "One moment, I'd think it was my fault you couldn't be that natural with me, the next I resented you for not granting me the same openness you gave Jalal. All the time I was seething with the need to bring it up. But what would I have said? I want you to *like* me not just love me? I need you to crave my company and companionship, outside of bed? What if all I managed was make you realize I didn't appeal to you in any way but sexually?"

Her heart lurched to another level of agitation. She'd never suspected he could have felt anything like this…

"Then I found out you were faltering in your studies. The fact that I didn't learn about it from you made me so…angry. I considered only what that meant to me, said about us, rather than how the problem itself impacted you."

That's more like it.

Her teeth ground together. "Another example of what made you the icon for self-absorbed sons of bitches everywhere."

He continued to stare at her with that still, searing intensity. "Jalal believed it was due to my…disruptive influence. I didn't know how to stop being disruptive without giving you up, or at least moving back to Zohayd and seeing you sporadically. I thought if he was right, you'd eventually come to the same conclusion. And if you did, you would be forced to make a choice between your progress and me. I feared it wouldn't be me you'd choose. I knew it shouldn't be. That's why I kept putting off bringing it up."

Everything froze inside her as if to stop the influx of new information that threatened to pulverize her long-held beliefs.

"It's also why I remembered the damn bet every single second I was with you. Not because I was afraid of losing to Jalal. Because I was afraid of losing you."

The stillness inside her trembled on the verge of shattering.

But wait—*wait!* Her view of him, of the past, was too well entrenched. It couldn't be changed with a few words…

But were they only words? Or reality? She'd already conceded Haidar hadn't been guilty of feeling nothing in Rashid's case, but feeling too much to be able to show it.

Had he been the same with her?

What if this was his problem across the board? Not that he'd inherited his mother's heartlessness and twisted, obsessive affection for the two people she considered extensions of herself, but only simulated it by his inability to expose his heart?

It would still make any involvement with him impossible, but it *would* rewrite his character, their whole history.

But…he was exposing his heart now, had been *communicating* with her, as she'd never thought he could. What if he'd matured into overcoming his emotional limitations?

As if reading her mind, he said, "Not that never sharing my fears or insecurities with you did any good. I lost you anyway."

If this was the truth, then what she'd said to him, how she'd walked out on him, must have pulverized his pride, his heart. As she'd thought he'd done hers.

Could she— *Dared* she believe?

But what else could she do? There was no reason he'd have said any of that if it weren't true.

Pain crashed over her.

God…what she'd cost them both.

Dejection receded, leaving his face blank. "I had it all planned from that first time I—pardon my presumption—claimed you. I intended us to be together while I worked to establish my success, while you did yours. The logistics of being in Azmahar when my base of operations was ideally Zohayd, of keeping our intimacies secret while being under the microscope of fame and notoriety, drove me to distraction. But I knew we needed to deepen our bond, protect it from intrusions, before we faced what the world would throw at us. With my mother, and your mother's position, with my mixed bag of problems, I knew it would be a lot."

She wanted to scream for him to stop.

He went on. "It was a mess, but I thought the passion we shared made up for the drawbacks. I thought you thought that, too. And though I didn't believe in my ability to make anyone happy, when you claimed to love me, you gave me hope that you saw in me what I didn't. I thought you'd give me the time I needed to trust myself with the new feelings, the unknown needs, the terrible vulnerability. But you didn't."

"Haidar…"

Her plaintive objection faltered. He was right. She hadn't. It suddenly no longer mattered why she hadn't. The fact remained.

The flow of his bitterness continued. "All these years, I rationalized your parting words, excused them. Excused you. I told myself that you lashed out when you saw me out of control emotionally for the first time and feared I'd turn morbidly possessive and controlling. I told myself you had every reason to worry with the gross imbalance of power between us. I kept thinking I must have scared you, made you say what you did to ensure I wouldn't come after you, never stopped imagining how it could have been if I hadn't. I never accepted that the woman I loved considered me a banal adventure. I never believed, not in my heart, that you never loved me at all."

Before she could cry that his heart had seen what had been in hers, he went on, "Now I have to accept that you never did. At the first test, you proved it. What you heard me say could have been interpreted in different ways. You chose the worst one. You'd already condemned me based on the word of your declared enemy. You didn't think me worth the chance to defend myself. All you thought of was how to protect your pride, how to avenge yourself. As if I'd been your enemy all along, not the man you claimed to love."

The urge to say something, anything, mushroomed inside her chest, felt it would rupture it. But anything she said now would be too little, too late.

He wasn't finished. "You have been treating me as your enemy, your only enemy even, since I reappeared in your life. I've been blaming my own actions again and hoping your intense desire proved you felt something real and powerful for me. But it seems you told me the truth only once. I *was* your exotic fling. You dressed it in higher emotions to feel justified in indulging in it, but in truth, you weren't ready to give me anything but stolen hours of pleasure. You didn't even give me what you would have granted any stranger—the right to be considered innocent until proven guilty. Whatever I was guilty of—the reticence and the jealousy and the inability to deal with the weakness my feelings for you engendered in me—I didn't warrant that punishment. But you don't even consider it punishment. You believe it's what I deserve."

She held back tears and self-recriminations. It wasn't time to give in to them. But she had to say something even if it was deficient.

He wouldn't let her. "But I don't accept your verdict, Roxanne. Whatever I was guilty of, I won't take all the blame. I'm sick and tired of being the one everyone demonizes. I will no longer think it okay for the people who once claimed to love me to see my every action in the worst light." His eyes flared with the molten steel of fury. "And I will no longer be held responsible for my mother's actions or accept being considered interchangeable with her character. I am not only her son. I am also my father's. But the thing that matters most is, I am *me*."

Before she could draw another breath, he turned around. Shocked to her core, she watched him cross the room that every brushstroke and article said he'd had done for her, having so accurately read her intensely personal fantasies.

She'd rejected him again in the setting he'd prepared for her with such thought and care.

At the double doors he stopped, turned, buttoning his shirt in deliberate moves. "My mother always told me that no one will love me but her, and to trust no one. Every time I disregarded her wisdom, I lost something vital. You, Jalal, Rashid. But it's clear the loss was always one-sided. You are all far better off without me." His eyes filled with bitter irony. "But I didn't get where I am by clinging to losing propositions. I'll accept that the problem lies within me and deal with it." He finished doing up his shirt, nothing left in his eyes but frozen steel. "So like I told them, I'll tell you. I'm getting the hell out of your life. This time, I'm staying out."

Eight

"Wow. Just...Wow."

Roxanne squeezed her eyes shut. She didn't want to see the incredulity, or the pity, in her companion's eyes.

She was already sorry she'd told Cherie anything.

It had been about four hours since Haidar had walked out of that bedroom. She'd gone after him, but had soon realized he'd left the estate. Haleem, the driver he'd flown in especially for her, had been waiting to take her home.

She'd held on until she'd gotten there. But the moment she'd seen Cherie, it had all come flooding out. The tears, and the whole story.

Cherie's exclamations didn't show signs of stopping any time soon. "I mean, dude...*wow*. And I thought *my* love life was complicated. Roxy, babe, you got the market cornered on complex messes."

Roxanne opened her eyes, exhaled her corroboration. "Yeah."

"And it seems 'tis open season for the destruction of long-held misconceptions. Me with Ayman, you with Prince Haidar. *Man,* you really have a *prince* for a lover!"

Refraining from amending it to *ex*-lover, Roxanne sighed again. "And for eight years I cherished my grudge against him. Then he tears into me with his side of the story, and here I am."

Cherie's eyes filled with seriousness and sympathy. "You must be feeling pretty stupid right now, huh?"

She grimaced in self-deprecation. "Not the description I would have used. Rash, overreacting, insecure, vindictive. But yeah, stupid works, too. Actually sums up all the above."

Cherie gave a bitter snicker. "You and me both. Since I came here, it's been dawning on me daily what an oversensitive moron I was with Ayman. You think it's something we picked up when we were in university together? We both started seeing our men then, and after a period of head-over-heels bliss, you walked out on yours, while I've been on a constant roller coaster with Ayman, mostly my doing. It's a wonder your man even tried to hook up with you again. It's a wonder mine married me and hasn't divorced me." The light blue of her eyes darkened with regret and despondence. "Especially after this last flounce."

"You still love him."

"God, yes. I love him so much it's what screws me up."

"You haven't told me exactly what went wrong between you."

Cherie rolled her eyes. "I'm a messy, outspoken-in-all-wrong-things, emotionally reticent pain in the butt, that's what went wrong."

"And you came here blaming him for being an anal, sanctimonious, overemotional jerk. Now you've switched to shouldering all the blame. I bet there's a middle ground here."

Cherie arched a delicate blond brow at her. "Like it exists in your situation?"

"Touché. But in yours, I can tell you that no matter what, he'd rather have your mess over perfection in a life without you. When I talked to him on the phone, he said, quote, 'Cherie's hell is better than anyone else's heaven,' unquote."

Tears poured down Cherie's cheeks as she collapsed back on the couch. "And of course he tells *you* that!"

"He's been trying to tell you. And he knew I'd transmit his words. So what are you going to do?"

Cherie leaned forward, burying her face in her hands. "I don't want him to put up with me and ruin his life. I want him to have the children he craves. I want him to let me go."

Roxanne scooted over, hugged her. "He doesn't want to let you go. He said he'll do anything to get you back. But have you ever told him what you just told me?"

Cherie raised drenched, smirking eyes. "Which part of emotionally reticent didn't you get?" Roxanne vented a frustrated breath. Cherie echoed it. "One thing we share is, we both pretended to jump because we thought we'd eventually be pushed. But we basically have the opposite of each other's problems. Ayman has always been the one pouring out his heart, and I'm the one who holds back and wisecracks his butt off. While your prince—excuse me again as I boggle over this—you really have a *prince!*" *Had* a prince. Roxanne bit back the correction. "And he was the one who had a glitch in his express-show machine. While you expressed yourself only too well, but only on your terms. So when he needed you to do it on his, tell him you were Team Haidar all the way, you didn't act on your professed love, proving it never existed."

Roxanne plopped back, hands grabbing her head in frustration. "Go ahead. Put it in an even worse light than he did."

Cherie grimaced apologetically. "I'm just sympathizing with someone who shares my inability to gush about my love. At least, *to* the object of my love. I get him."

A spasm pinched her heart. "And I'm only beginning to get him. When it's too late."

It was Cherie's turn to hug her. "Do you have an Azmaharian mother-in-law breathing down your man's neck to discard you and get a model that will provide the required brood? Do you have a terminal disorderliness disorder and live with a neatness freak? Do you have five years of marriage behind you, and you're at the point where you think the only man you'll ever love is better off without your baggage and shortcomings? If you answer no to all the above, you've got it easy, lady."

"Put that way, my problems seem trivial in comparison. Except for one tiny point. Your man wants you back. Mine doesn't."

"Sure he does. He's been holding a torch for you for eight years even after you seemingly pulverized his heart and pride."

"Now he's blown out said torch."

"He's hurt and he's sulking. But one thing for sure. This guy has never run after anything or anyone. He's a high-and-mighty prince-*cum*-god, for Pete's sake. And he's gone against everything in his nature and done all the running in your relationship. He's in dire need for you to go after him this time."

"What if he says to leave him the hell alone?"

Cherie jumped up, and wonder of wonders, started gathering her cups and plates. "Here's what we'll both do. I'll open up to Ayman, and you'll go after Haidar. It *is* a definite danger neither maneuver will work. Are we going to let that stop us from trying?"

Roxanne had started thinking this was a terrible idea. Hours ago. Now she knew it was the worst one she'd ever cooked up.

Even Cherie hadn't thought she'd go this far. She'd thought she'd only go as far as calling Haidar, beg for face time.

She'd texted Haidar instead, *told* him when and where to meet her. She'd thought if she was doing this, she might as well go all out. In a blaze of glorious recklessness.

Not that it was working. She'd been waiting for eight hours.

She'd made allowances for everything that could hold him up. If he meant to come. Every minute after the fifth hour when no more excuses sufficed had felt like sandpaper being dragged over her raw nerves, every one telling her she'd just dialed his outrage higher with her presumption.

Even if she hadn't, why would he want to see her again? He'd made up his mind that he'd heard all he needed to hear from her. She no longer had a right to his indulgence or patience, which he'd been showering her with since he'd showed up in her life again.

Her phone rang.

She fumbled with it as if it were a squirming fish, hit Answer, put it to her ear, heart turned inside out.

"Kaif hallek, ya azeezati?"

At hearing the drawled *How are you, my dearest,* the detonation of disappointment made her cover the mic to groan. *Jalal.*

Why was she so surprised? He'd called her half a dozen times a day ever since that first meeting. They'd made quite the headway in his campaign at first. But since her confrontation with Haidar a week ago, only her word to Jalal had made her work on his case at all. That and the need to get everything out of the way so she could obsess over Haidar with her full focus.

Wanting this over with, she skimmed the niceties. "Have you checked your in-box? I sent you the demographic analysis."

"Aih, I saw them." From the brief pause, Jalal had noticed her haste. As gentlemanly as ever, he glossed over it. "Brilliant work. I don't know what I would have done without you. You have incredible insight."

She almost scoffed. *Selective* insight was more like it. When it came to Haidar, she'd had that in the negative values.

"But this isn't a business call," Jalal said. "You weren't looking as well as usual a couple of days ago."

And you're not doing me any favors worrying.

Out loud she said, "Work is too much sometimes."

"If my side of it is weighing you down…"

She did wish, for so many reasons, she'd never promised to be Jalal's advisor. But she had given her word. She would abide by it. "No, really. Just don't worry, okay?"

"If you're sure." He sounded very unsure himself.

Quit the big-brother probing, already, she almost screamed.

He made it worse. "I heard you've seen a lot of Haidar."

And I want to see a lot more of him, all of him. But I'm not telling you that, or where I am now, or what I'm trying to do.

"You didn't mention our arrangement," he probed.

"No." Even if she wasn't bound to secrecy by her word to Jalal, it had never occurred to her when she was with Haidar. Nothing else existed when he was around.

"I was hoping you wouldn't tell him I'm in Azmahar."

That was strange. "But he must know you're here."

"He doesn't. My appearance at your door evidently wasn't as dramatic as his. I'm not as dramatic in general here as he is. Wearing an Aal Shalaan face comes in very handy in avoiding unwanted attention in Azmahar."

So Jalal was being covert. She could see the merit in that, for the info-gathering stage. But why wouldn't he want Haidar to know of his presence? Did he fear his brother would try to sabotage him? Would Haidar go that far in his rivalry?

"I didn't tell you everything about our last confrontation." When Haidar told Jalal he renounced their very blood tie. "I accused him of being our mother's accomplice in her conspiracy to take Zohayd apart."

Shock screeched through her, made her choke, "B-but Haidar was the one who discovered where she hid the jewels, brought the conspiracy to an end."

"I know. But…there were unexplained activities between him and our mother, extensive amounts of money he'd given her. I asked him about it, and he told me what I could do with my suspicions. I ended up accusing him of only pretending to help us when she was exposed so that he'd appear innocent, that she agreed to play along, since she'd do anything to protect him. I said he manipulated me emotionally until he had me begging with him for her exile instead of imprisonment, and that they were both only biding their time until they came up with another plot to put him on the throne."

She staggered to the nearest flat surface, the ledge of the pier, plopped down on it.

This was…unthinkable. Could it possibly…

No. She wasn't doing this again. She wasn't thinking the worst of Haidar again. Not without giving him every benefit of the doubt first, giving him the chance to explain his side.

But what mattered here was one thing. "You believe this?"

"No." One single word laden with a world full of regret and pain. "But I'm not the collected man you know when it comes to Haidar, not even exactly sane. I was livid, thinking what our mother could have caused, for him. It was impossible, with him being so reticent, to separate my rage with her from him. He was indirectly responsible for everything she'd done, and I wanted to punch him with my accusations until he lashed back, opened up, told me everything, shared with me fully again, if just this once. He didn't. He just walked away."

As he had from her. Seemed he was an expert at that.

But again, what had seemed to be such a callous action had only been an outraged reaction. Haidar had walked away from the twin who, when a real test was forced on him, had behaved as if Haidar had always been his worst enemy. As she had.

It felt weird to change her perspective, see her admired friend as the offender. Seemed Haidar did manage to force out the passionate side in others—their best and worst.

Suddenly, she felt a presence behind her.

Her heart almost fired from her ribs.

"Sorry, gotta go. Talk later," was all she said to Jalal, barely heard his surprised agreement before she ended the call.

She took a shuddering breath before she rose, swung around.

If it was Haleem, she might shove him into the sea.

It wasn't. It was Haidar.

He came.

He was walking toward her from the end of the terrace that extended into a stone passage that traversed the sandy beach. It transformed into a wooden pier that forged into the bay, widened at its end into the circular platform where she was standing.

In seconds he was stepping onto the platform she'd ringed with candles blazing in crimson quartz holders. He glowed like the desert god that he was as he passed between the brass torches she'd lit, their incandescent flames undulating in the calm breeze, accentuating his every feature and line. In all black with the only relief a shirt the color of his eyes, he took her breath away, sent her heart into hyperdrive. Her every nerve quivered at beholding his magnificence, at entering his orbit. Her every sense ignited with no-longer-suppressed responses and emotions.

He transferred his expressionless gaze from her to the candles, to the buffet table at the end of the platform, and finally to the table for two she'd arranged in its center.

He looked back at her. "I see you've invaded and occupied my home."

She shivered as his voice, impassive like his expression, flowed down her nervous pathways like warm molasses.

She'd expected him to comment on her setup. Seemed where he was concerned, the only given was to expect the unexpected.

She licked her dry, tingling lips. "Just your pier."

He came to a stop four steps away, went so still he looked

like a statue of a titan, the only animate things about him his satin mane sifting around his leonine head, his clothes rustling around his steel-fleshed frame.

Then he shoved his hands into his pockets, the epitome of tranquillity. "I thought we agreed we were better off staying off each other's properties and out of each other's lives."

She held back from closing the gap between them with all she had. "We did. Just not at the same time. Or for the same reasons."

"The sequence or cause of coming to this vital decision isn't important. As long as we both reached it."

"Problem is, once you did, I unreached it."

His gaze lengthened, the gentle rumble of the sea lapping the shore deepening his silence. Then without moving, or changing his expression or tone, he said, "I'm not playing this game, Roxanne."

"It's not a game. I never played games with you."

"Could have fooled me."

"I actually could and should have known you better." She took a step closer. "The problem is, we fell into bed too soon. Once we did, it was impossible for us to have one nonhormonally overwrought thought or reaction where the other was concerned."

One dense, slanting eyebrow rose. "You're saying you chose to believe the worst about me because passion made you unable to think straight?"

"Why so skeptical? You admitted to about the same. As a friend pointed out, we suffered from a communication disorder. My verbal-but-not-about-my-issues kind was as bad as your nonverbal one."

He brooded down at her, clearly unconvinced.

She tried a new angle. "You thought it a possibility I'd think of Jalal while I was with you. I thought *you* thought of Jalal while you were with me. We're guilty of the same stupidity, each in our own uniquely stupid way. So how about we call it even?"

That imperious eyebrow rose again. "You really like to say that, don't you?"

Her heart shook at the first ray of change in his expression. "And when I last said that, you said we're not, not by an eight-year-long shot. I believe that now."

He went totally still again. The steel of his eyes seemed to catch the torch fire, singeing her.

"What do you want, Roxanne?"

She shook with the sheer, leashed intensity in that question. He needed her to spell it out. She was only too happy to.

"I want you. I only ever wanted you."

And he moved, away, restored the distance she'd managed to obliterate. "So all you needed to change your mind was me deciding to stop pursuing you? And you realizing I meant it?"

"If you're saying I'm coming after you because you pose a challenge now, *et'tummen*…rest easy. That doesn't even figure into this."

His eyes narrowed to silver lasers. It had once aroused him to near savagery when she'd spoken Arabic to him.

"So what does? My little speech before I walked out?"

Her nod was difficult as her rate of melting quickened, her body readying itself for the onslaught of his passion. "That little speech was sure eye-opening. And heart-wrenching. I spent eight years never once thinking you had a side of the story."

"Are you saying if you faced me then, screamed bloody betrayal, and I'd told you said side, none of this would have happened?"

"No," she had to admit. "I trusted you and what we had too little. And if you, the man who never opened up to me during the year of our involvement, suddenly had, I would have thought you were placating me to carry on your bet."

"So it's because you believe the bet is no longer on, and only because I no longer talk to Jalal, that you believe me now."

"No, again. I believe you because we've grown up and out of our inability to talk to each other. We've been communicating for real during those verbal duels. And you let me see your vulnerability and emotions for the first time. It made me realize I dehumanized you, even when I was claiming to love you. Then I demonized you when I thought you'd never loved me."

Silence stretched until she thought he wouldn't talk again.

Suddenly he moved. "I accept your peace offering. Let's eat."

Her mouth fell open as he passed her.

Once at the table, in perfect grace and control, he took the chair she'd meant for him, his back to the sea. She'd wanted the lights from the house and grounds to join the pier's in illuminating him. He propped one forearm on the table and sat relaxed, majestic, sweeping the buffet table where serving plates simmered on gentle flames that danced in the balmy sea breeze.

He panned his gaze back to her with ultimate serenity as she stopped across the table. "You will serve me, won't you?"

She narrowed her eyes at him, her lips struggling not to spread in delight. "Don't push your luck."

His lips twitched, too. His eyes remained unfathomable.

Turning around, she headed to the buffet table, her heart dancing a jig inside her. He was letting her back in.

As she adorned their plates with an assortment of appetizers, he called out, "Do hurry. The aromas are too mouthwatering."

Her steps back to him were measured, to rein in the urge to plop the plates down, charge him, straddle and devour *him*.

She came behind him, leaned to place his plate before him, let her breasts brush his back, her hair fall over his shoulder. "All delicious things come to he who doesn't rush the chef."

He tilted his head, turning his face partially toward her, his eyes downcast. She felt she might fall over him with the dizziness his scent and heat induced. Which might not be a bad thing…

He reached for his napkin, flapped it open. "Don't tell me you cooked all this."

She straightened like a malfunctioning robot, her body buzzing, her legs rubbery after the contact that had backfired, having no effect on him, but managing to flare her arousal.

"Why so shocked? I can handle myself in a kitchen." She struggled not to fall in a heap in her chair. "But you're right. I didn't. I did a lot of the work, but I was mainly following the directions of the one who designed the meal. Cherie is an incredible artist, in cooking and in many other forms of art."

He only nodded, started to eat with gusto.

After he polished off the appetizers and the two courses of the meal, and she watched him eat while trying to draw him into conversation, he looked up. "Your friend should consider a catering business. I'd be a regular customer."

She grinned, delighted that she'd pleased him, that he appreciated Cherie and her efforts. Even if he didn't include her directly in his praise. "She'll be thrilled you think so. She almost fainted when she saw your kitchen. When she set foot here, really. She still can't believe that she cooked for a prince. That I even know you."

His eyes darkened. "She knows how well you…know me?"

"She knows how well I…knew you. And didn't know you at all. She also knows how much I want to know you, in every way, now."

Another of those silences that engulfed that wide-open night, magnified every ripple of water, every whistle of wind, every beat of her heart, lengthened.

Suddenly he pushed his chair back, stood up. "That was a lovely meal, Roxanne. My most sincere compliments to the chef. I accept your…amends. Best of luck finding the same success in your endeavors to put Azmahar back on track."

She gaped at him as he turned around and strode away.

That was it? He was walking away again? This time on good terms instead of terrible ones?

But she couldn't let him walk away again. She wouldn't.

She scrambled up. "But I haven't *really* made…amends yet."

He stopped. After another endless moment, he looked over his shoulder. "No, you haven't, have you?"

Then with one last look of supreme indifference, he turned and strode away like a lion would from the prey he'd just feasted on.

It took only heartbeats for delight and determination to overcome agitation and hesitation. It was as clear as the starlit sky he wanted her to run after him some more.

She had no problem with that. She couldn't wait to do it. She would run after him, and she would catch him, if it took the rest of her life.

Nine

Haidar didn't slow down, didn't look back.

The only way to catch up with him would be to sprint. She didn't. He wanted to keep the distance between them.

She let him keep it. All the way to his bedroom.

He strode through the open double doors, disappeared inside.

A smile trembled on her lips as she stopped across the threshold. Why not let him wonder for a bit?

But it was she who couldn't last. She was dying to have him.

She entered the antechamber, swerved into the room…and gaped.

Haidar was reclining at the dark emerald damask couch by the balcony doors, legs stretched out on it, his jacket discarded, his shirt partially undone. And he was reading a book.

He didn't raise his head from his apparent engrossment as she approached him. He let her come within touching distance before he slowly, and without moving a thing, swept his gaze up to her.

"Anything I can do for you?"

His low, dark rumble spread through her, dried her mouth, melted everything else.

In response, she let her shawl slip. "Everything, actually. And not just for me. To me. With me."

His gaze singed down her face, following the autumn leaves–colored silk as it slithered to the ground. On the way, he took note of the sensuality and delicacy of her spaghetti-strap dress. On his way up, his gaze lingered on the breasts now swollen and snug against the top. By the time he came back to her eyes, she was shivering with need, as if he'd caressed her within an inch of sanity.

Instead of reaching for her, he closed his book, relaxed back on the couch, still holding her prisoner to his fathomless scrutiny. So she reached for him.

Bracing a knee on the couch, arousal thundering through her, her hands trembled as they roamed the incredible breadth of his chest. He held her eyes as she moaned at the acuteness of sensations that touching him jolted through her. The intimidating bulge in his pants got impossibly bigger. But the moment she started pulling his shirt out, fumbling with its buttons, her forearms were clamped in inescapable sinew-and-bone manacles.

"You've made those kinds of…amends before." His eyes crackled with what felt like the advance bolts of a devastating storm. He pushed her arms away as he sat up and was off the couch in one of those miraculously effortless moves. "I'm not interested in an encore along the same lines."

She collapsed on the couch, looked up at him as he stood before her, perfect down to his last pore.

He would make a perfect king. Probably the only kind that could save Azmahar now.

He was *her* perfect man. The only one she'd ever want. Or love. Whatever happened, wherever this led, or didn't lead, she belonged to him, heart and soul.

Now if he'd only hurry and claim her body, too.

She rose on precarious legs. "Not that I *was* offering anything along the same lines, but what kind of amends do *you* have in mind?"

Another stormy silence as his probing invaded her recesses.

Then, distinct, slow, annihilating, he drawled, "Surrender. Full, unconditional. And irretrievable."

She almost came right there and then.

This man *was* out to take revenge on her.

Her whole body throbbed like one inflamed nerve. Her core spasmed with the near release he'd driven her to with the force of his intention.

In answer, she pushed her dress straps off her shoulder, reached back to undo its zipper, let the silk sigh to her feet like the shed petals of an alien, emerald flower.

Facing him in only her strapless bra, thong and stilettos, she said a breathless "Done."

His eyes flared with a fierceness that almost knocked her off her feet. His gaze ravaged a path of almost frightening hunger over her, sending her heart flailing with trepidation, almost had her howling with anticipation. He still made no move.

He needed a more definitive demonstration.

She turned on jellified legs toward the bed in the middle of the room that he'd designed in echoes of her complexion. She climbed on top, spread out in its center and held out her arms to him.

He moved then. Before her heart could stumble over a few beats, he was at the foot of the bed, looking down at her spread out before him.

"You will give me everything this time, Roxanne. Everything you have. Everything you are. Everything you didn't think you had to give. If you withhold anything, I will take nothing."

"Everything." Her nod was frantic. "And I want your everything in return."

Something savage blossomed in his gaze. "You know what you're asking for?"

He was demanding more than her body. He'd soon find out he had all of her, through and through.

She struggled to her elbows, meeting his menace with her trust, her vow, her determination. "Oh, yes."

He suddenly clamped her feet, dragged her by them, slid her across the satiny sheets. One hand took one of hers, tugged, bringing her slamming into his flesh.

"I want to invade you, brand you, devour you whole." She gasped her willingness for anything he'd do to her, tried to wrap herself around him. "But you'll have to wait for that."

A flip had her back in the middle of the bed, lying on her stomach. A firm hand at the small of her back kept her down. She resisted him enough to remain propped on her elbows, so she could watch him as he slid up her body, nipping and kneading his way from the soles of her feet to her nape, ridding her of her panties and bra on the way, leaving her with only her sandals on.

He worshipped her with his ferocity, owned her with his voracity. Every dig of his fingers in her flesh had the exact force, each nip of his teeth the exact roughness to extract maximum pleasure from every nerve ending. He layered sensations with each press and bite until she felt devoured and assimilated, until she was overloading.

Something was charring inside her. She undulated back against him in a fever, pressing her clamoring flesh against any part of him in mindless pursuit of assuagement. "*Arjook*, Haidar…"

At her cried-out plea, in Arabic, he growled something and flatted her beneath him. She lay there, naked, her every nerve abraded by the sensation of his flesh through his clothes, quaking at the domination of his heated bulk, at each wholly arousing touch.

"*Maafi raja*…no pleas, *ya naari,* only possession."

His breath burned her cheek, its scent filling her lungs, and everything inside her snapped. She cried out, twisted on her back, surged up to cling around him, to his lips in desperate kisses.

"Eight years, Roxanne," he growled inside her mouth between the tongue thrusts that filled her, conquered her. "Do you know how many times I cursed you for depriving me of this?"

He transferred his lips to her neck and shoulders, tasting every tremor strumming through her as his hands slid down her body, tormented every fiber into a riot of sensation. He dragged a rough, electrocuting hand between her thighs, kneaded and tormented his way to her core. The heel of his thumb ground against her outer lips at the same moment the wet furnace of his mouth clamped over a throbbing nipple. Sensation slashed her nerves.

He dealt her another blow as his deft fingers spread her, probed her readiness, two sliding between her engorged, molten inner lips, stilling at her entrance. She flailed, whimpered, arched up into his hand.

"Do you know what kind of frustration I suffered, wanting to see you like this, to feel you on fire, hunger shaking you apart? How I yearned to do this…"

Those long, sure fingers plunged inside her. Her hips bucked, her squeal morphing into a shriek when he pumped into her in slow in-out glides, filling her, beckoning at her inner trigger. He growled his satisfaction as her slick flesh gripped back at him, tried to wring its release from his torment.

"And do you know how it felt being *unable* to do this? Thinking I'd never own your flesh like this again?"

Sensation rocketed, more at the emotion and passion fueling his words than at his expert pleasuring. She keened, opened herself wider for him, needing pleasure any way he gave it, offering her surrender.

"You can have it all now," she gasped. "And always."

"Saherah." His growl singed her, even as his thumb stroked her tight, nerve-filled bud in rhythmic circles, the exact pressure and speed she needed, escalating her need for release with each stroke. He swallowed every tremulous word, every tear until she was on the verge of shuddering apart. Then he let up.

She knew what he was doing. He was punishing her. By building up to an eventual, fiercer reward.

Her body felt it would combust if he didn't push her over the edge. But this was a test of the extent of her surrender. Letting him give her more than she could dream of, his way.

Before she could verbalize her submission, he slid down to lay on his stomach between her thighs, draping her legs over his back.

"And do you know what I suffered, craving the taste of you, knowing I'd never know it again?"

He inhaled her, rumbled like a lion maddened by the scent of his female, blew a gust of acute sensation over her quivering flesh. Her vision disappeared in a haze of crimson lust as he latched his hot lips over her intimate ones, plunging her into a vortex of need. He eased his fingers back into her, his tongue joining in, licked from where they were buried inside her upward, circling until she was sobbing feverishly. No pleas, though. Just confessions of what he was doing to her.

When he'd heard enough, taken her to the edge and dragged her back panting and shuddering enough times, he nipped her, knowing exactly where, how hard.

She convulsed, bucked, smashed her flesh to his mouth, opening herself fully to his double sensual assault, each glide and graze and thrust sending hotter lances skewering through her, pleasure slamming through her in desperate surges. Her climax wrung her out of satisfaction. He growled, drank every drop, kept pushing her, plumbing her flesh for more, until she tumbled from the explosive peak, drained, sated. Stupefied.

Had he ever driven her to such ecstasy?

Sight seeping back, her drugged eyes sought his, as if for answers. They sparkled in the ingeniously placed and calibrated lighting of the room and that of the oil lamps she'd lit, heavy with hunger and gratification.

As if to answer her, he said, "It's merciful, for both of us, time dulled even my memories. Either that or you have matured from a craving into an addiction."

Pride, delight surged, at his confession, at the sight of a long-craved fantasy. Him, clothed, between her legs, her, naked, splayed open over his Herculean shoulders.

Her hands trembled through his lush hair. "Look who's talking."

He chuckled against her inner thighs, cupped her, desensitizing her before he came up, prowled over her prostrate body on all fours like the sexy beast he was.

He straddled her hips, started stripping. That got her mind rebooting, her muscles functioning. She had to be the one to expose him. She raised her hands, only to have them join her thighs in the prison of his. "Your amends are *far* from made."

He licked his lips as if still tasting her, tormenting her with his slow striptease, tightening his knees around her thighs and hands, deepening her helplessness, winding her pounding into a tighter rhythm. She almost relinquished the rules of surrender, to beg to touch and taste him, almost passed out with the pressure of need.

He stood up on the bed, got rid of his pants and boxers in one move. Her senses swam, her mouth watered, the spike of hunger, the pinch of intimidation, the need to feel his daunting manhood, smell it, taste it almost pulling her under.

But she'd had her chance a week ago. He would punish her for that stunt by denying her the pleasure for a period only he would determine. He also had other ways of exacting payment.

He came down over her, pressed his erection to her belly. Feeling the marble smooth and hard column of hot flesh against hers made her writhe, gasp. It awed her that she'd accommodated all that inside her. The remembered sensations as he'd occupied her, stretched her into mindlessness, made her arch up seeking more. He ground harder into her, his knees splaying her thighs, his silk-sprinkled chest teasing her aching nipples.

The moment he crushed her beneath him, she wrapped herself around him, buried her face in his neck, opened her lips over his pulse. Every steel muscle expanded, bunched, buzzed. She whimpered at the relief of his weight on her, the feel of his power, the taste and texture of his flesh beneath her lips, the sheer delight of breathing him in.

"Do you know the depth of longing that preyed on me, needing you beneath me like this? Do you know how much of my sanity I lost wanting to be inside you, yearning to have you around me? Knowing I was destined for starvation?"

His bass groans had regret and agony for the lost years clotting in her heart. *"Haidar, habibi, kamm ana aasfah..."*

At hearing her calling him her love, saying how sorry she was, his hands convulsed in her hair, pinned her for the full vehemence of his passion. His lips crashed on hers, silencing her, wrenching keens from her with scorching, desperate kisses. He lifted her off the bed, one hand supporting her head for his ravaging, the other at her back, holding her for his chest to torment her breasts, driving her into more of a frenzy. Her eyes streamed tears from the emotional and carnal torment. What she'd cost them...

He touched the head of his erection to her entrance, nudged

her, bathing himself in her desire. "*Guleeli, ya naari*—tell me you know, Roxanne. Tell me you suffered the same."

She pressed his biceps convulsively, arched for his completion. "I know. And I did. I suffer worse now…"

His eyes roiled with a dizzying mixture of ferociousness and tenderness. "As you should. Now, *ya naari,* for all the years without your inferno, your solace, now you *pay*."

He pumped his hips, pushing against her entrance. Though she was melting with readiness, it had always taken a measure of force for him to breach her. His eyes blazed with the need to forge inside her. Her frantic nod begged for the no-holds-barred invasion.

He lunged, was there, where she needed him, penetrating her in one forceful thrust.

The expansion of her tissues around his erection was so sudden, the fullness sharpened into pain that exploded into pleasure so fierce, darkness danced at the periphery of her vision.

She gasped, thrashed. His face clenched with something like agony as he stilled, started to withdraw. She clung to him as she would to a raft as she drowned.

"Eight years' worth," she sobbed. "Take it all now…*now*."

"*Aih, ya naari,* take it all, give it back to me." He refilled her, his tongue thrusting inside her mouth with the same ferocity.

His growls grew dark as he gave her what she'd been disintegrating for, in the exact force and pace. He invaded her, stretched her more with each plunge, forging deeper, the head of his shaft sliding against her internal flesh, setting off a string of discharges that buried her under layers of sensations.

It all felt maddeningly familiar, yet totally new, a buildup that seemed to originate from her every cell and radiate from his own at once, distilling desperation into a physical symptom.

Then everything compacted into one unendurable moment that detonated outward. She shattered.

She heaved so hard she almost lifted him in the air, her flesh pulsing around his so fiercely she couldn't breathe, not for the first dozen clenches of excruciating pleasure.

"Aih, ya naari, pay for all my suffering with your pleasure."

His rumble snapped something inside her, flooded air into her lungs. She screamed and screamed her ecstasy as he rode her, his hardness pistoning satisfaction into her.

"Roxanne…" He rose above her, muscles bulging, eyes tempestuous, supernatural in beauty. He threw his head back and roared her name as every muscle in his body locked, his erection lodging against her womb, jetting his own release in long, hard surges, setting off her deepest triggers in one more conflagration.

He fed her convulsions, pumping her to the last twitches of fulfillment until the world receded…

Roxanne stirred from the depths of bliss.

She opened her eyes and found herself staring at the breathtaking vista of the sea and the island outside Haidar's balcony. Contentment expanded inside her, had her turning toward him.

He wasn't there.

"Haidar?"

No answer. He must be in the shower. Or the kitchen. Or somewhere. Judging by the setting sun outside, she'd been knocked out for the last twelve hours. Or maybe even thirty-six.

But that was his fault. He'd taken the eight years' worth almost literally, exacted vengeance by ecstasy until she'd lost count. And consciousness.

She got out of bed, waddled to the bathroom, wincing at the soreness from his repeated possession. She needed to soak if she hoped to be ready for more.

She came out of the bath tingling with rejuvenation and anticipation, went in search of him.

She found him nowhere.

She called him. His phone was turned off.

Where was he? What could have made him disappear?

No answer made sense. As hours passed, terrible explanations started to trickle in, expand, take over rationalizations. That he'd taken her up on her offer but had never intended to stay for an encore. That last night had meant only two things to him—vindication, closure.

Was that it? He'd gotten them and just…left?

Unable to accept that verdict, she waited, every sound in the expansive house almost uprooting her heart with hope. But he didn't return.

Night had deepened to utter bleakness when she found herself walking to the pier, to the platform where she'd thought her life had started again.

She looked out to the island that was now an awe-striking shadow under the light of a nascent moon and blazing stars. She'd thought he'd take her there, to explore, to make love, to—

"I thought you'd be gone."

She spun around, saw him approaching through the liquid pain filling her eyes. The conquering lover, the devil-may-care prince, the challenging adversary were all gone.

A frozen man had replaced them all.

His eyes regarded her without a spark of the life or lust that had always filled them. His voice was as lifeless. "But then I thought many things and they all turned out to be wrong. Now I can no longer fool myself into believing what I wish to believe."

God, what did he mean?

He was telling her he couldn't forgive or forget? Worse,

that his injuries remained the same whether she'd meant to inflict them or not?

"So why did you stay? I thought we'd said everything."

Was this his real revenge? Give her miles of hope to wrap around her neck, then push her off her skyscraper of foolish dreams?

But he had to realize this wasn't just retribution. Whatever injury she'd caused him, he'd survived it. Thrived, even. Shattering her heart now wouldn't only be for the second time. It would be for the last. There would be no surviving it.

"If you stayed thinking I'd back down, I won't. I have to end this now, or there'll be no surviving it."

Had she spoken her thoughts out loud?

No. He just knew how much he was damaging her.

Not that she could blame him. He'd walked away, told her to go. She'd pursued him, planned and plotted her own destruction. She'd done this to herself, as she had in the past. No one had forced her to love him, give him more than he'd wanted. The first time she'd been too young, had had the delusion that she could love again, could come to life again with someone else. Now she'd grown up and out of her false hopes. Now she knew. She could only love, and live, if it was him, with him.

And he didn't want her.

Trembling so hard she could barely summon enough coordination to walk, she stumbled back toward him, wishing he would disappear so she wouldn't have to feel him this close one last time.

Then she was passing him, holding her breath so that his scent wouldn't twist the dagger of longing inside her chest. The stretch of the pier into land was ahead of her. The path to escape. To the nothingness that dominated her future…

She came to a jolting halt.

He'd stopped her.

Before she could cry for him to just "sever the artery and let it bleed out," as they said here, he took her by the shoulders.

She struggled to push his hands away. She couldn't *bear* this.

His eyes smoldered down at her as if he was in the grips of a fever. "I can't let you go, Roxanne. I thought I could, but I can't. I will take anything for as long as you will give it. And if you prefer, I won't bring up marriage again."

Ten

Bring up marriage? Again?

Roxanne stared up at Haidar, nothing making sense any-more.

His fingers convulsed on her shoulders. "I was an arrogant bastard, making it sound like a fait accompli. I deserved that 'shut up.' I shouldn't have gotten angry when you said it. I shouldn't have made it an ultimatum, shouldn't have said that it was marriage or nothing."

Every word out of his mouth pushed vague things from the periphery of her mind and into focus. Hazy snippets she might have heard as she'd drifted in and out of oblivion. His voice, hers, the words themselves evaporating like a dream after waking.

He was saying that, during those unremembered fragments, he'd proposed to her? That she'd answered his proposal with… *shut up?*

"If you stayed to tell me I'm an idiot, but that I can stop being one and take what you're willing to give me, I accept."

"Haidar, I don't—"

Suddenly he let her go, turned around to gaze into the star-blazing sky. "Your point-blank refusal reinforced once again that I've never been compatible with human relationships, a classic case of someone 'only a mother can love.' But it was trying to let you go that made me realize what I am guilty of."

"Haidar, you don't need—"

He swung back to her. "I *do* need to say this. In the past I compounded being jealous and suspicious with my uncompromising need to be in total control of myself, and to have every last heartbeat of you. I made it worse by being unable to share anything about myself, yet wanting you to know and accommodate my emotional needs the same way you did my physical ones. When you didn't, dared give appreciation and ease and laughter to Jalal, I got so mad, felt so hurt, that the part of me that is like my mother took over. I demanded more from you physically and withdrew further emotionally, trying to make you come closer to compensate. I made you believe that my feelings where you were concerned were at best not healthy. Believing they were nonexistent was a simple step from that."

She stepped closer, her mind churning. "You're saying you think you deserved my distrust after all?"

"I never said I didn't. I said I didn't deserve all the blame. You were to blame, too, claiming to love me for what I was, when you didn't know what *that* was. You didn't recognize that I was reaching out to you in the only way I knew how, showing you with all the effort and trouble I took to be with you how vital you were to me. I did reach out to you outright that day, begged you to reassure me."

He turned away, shoulders slumping as if all fight had gone out of him. "But you probably did yourself a favor by leaving. Last week, I didn't walk away only because I was feeling sorry for myself, but because I did think you'd be better off without me. I hurt you just by being who I am, even before you found out about that stupid bet, before I exposed you to my mother's abuse."

He turned back to her, his eyes fevered. "But you were right to reject me again. I said I would accept anything you were willing to give, but I won't. I can't. I was all or none in the past, and I haven't changed. When I came back to Azmahar I was in control of my tendencies because I was telling myself I now only wanted you. Then we had our confrontation, *then* last night happened—and that control is gone. I can't and won't be satisfied with less than all of you, forever. It might have sounded exciting to you in the heat of passion, when you thought I was talking about sex. But after you realized I meant everything for real…I don't blame you if that put you off."

"It doesn't," she whispered, the enormity of what he was revealing choking her. "Not if it's a two-way street…?"

His eyes narrowed, his body going still. "It is. You have all of me. If you'll only take it."

Havoc filled her eyes, quivered on her lips with the poignancy of letting go of doubts, seeing her way clear and sure, and permanent back to him. "The bad before the good, huh?"

The hope flaring in his eyes dimmed again. "That scares you?"

And she surged into him, hugged him with all her strength. "Not anymore. I trust you, Haidar. And if it took me a while to get there, it's because you're so full of contradictions, you made it almost impossible to know what you're all about. You also overwhelm me. Which kinda counteracts any attempts at being rational where you're concerned." She looked up at him, her heart in her eyes for him to see. "You were so unreadable I thought there was nothing to read beyond the obvious. You were so confident I thought you had no doubts, no weaknesses. The rest of your assets painted an inhuman paragon with no human failings or emotions. But mainly, you're so devastatingly…potent, I thought you'd never be satisfied with one woman. Hell, I thought you probably couldn't and shouldn't be."

He stiffened in her arms. "Unfaithfulness, let alone promiscuity, is one thing I don't suffer from."

Her smile trembled with all the joy settling in her heart. "I know that, now that I see you for who you really are. I thought you were domineering and controlling, but you're only dominant and in control. You're uncompromising, but you can be flexible where it matters. You seemed cruel, willing to get your way over anyone's dead body, but either you grew out of it, or you never actually walked over anyone who didn't deserve it. You're scarily serious about work, but it turns out you have this supreme ability to be fun and funny, too. And you have insecurities like the rest of us mortals, behind that impenetrable front. To top it all off, the harsh pragmatist in you shares your body with an incredible romantic."

His eyes were widening as she spoke. Now he swallowed. "You see good sides to me?"

"I see *fantastic* sides to you. But most important, they are fantastic to *me*. I would have loved you—I *have* loved you—for far, far less. I love you now for everything you are and aren't."

"But…you told me to shut up!"

She dived into his arms again, groaning. "I don't even remember saying it, but I probably meant the one thing I needed most in the world right then. For you to shut up and let me *sleep*."

He held her away, flabbergasted. "You mean I spent a day in a worse hell than any I have ever imagined because you were sleep-talking? *Ya Ullah*…when I said marriage or nothing, demanded a yes or no, you looked me straight in the eye, said an emphatic no, then turned your back and went to sleep."

"I probably would have said no if you'd asked me if I needed to breathe. You devastated me with your vengeance of ecstasy." She laughed, threw her arms around his neck and clung. "I think we can now say we have one of the most unique proposal tales on record."

His arms convulsed around her, his expression still jittery. "You can laugh. I was considering leaving civilization for good."

She cupped his cheek, reveling in the freedom, in the wonder of being able to show him everything in her heart at last. "Jumping to conclusions where the other is concerned seems to be what we do best."

"Aih." His frown was all dejected regret. Then determination blazed. "But never again. From now on, we never do that. Promise me you will always tell me anything at all."

She dragged him into a fierce kiss, laughing, tears flowing, murmured against his lips, "I promise."

He put her away again. "You *are* saying you want to marry me?"

"If it entails being with you for better or for worse, in sickness and in health, till death parts us and probably not even then, I do."

Haidar shook with the enormity of the averted catastrophe, of witnessing Roxanne's bliss and certainty. He needed to solidify their pact, their claim on each other. Right now.

He swept her up in his arms, didn't feel the ground beneath his feet on his way to their bedroom. His heart thundered as he put her down on the bed, tore at their clothes, unable to bear anything between them. Then he looked down at her, his sorceress, his goddess, in all her naked glory.

Her breasts were a feast, her waist nipped, making the flare of her hips fuller. Her limbs were firm and smooth, her shoulders square and strong. Every curve and line and swell of her was the translation of his every fantasy.

He skimmed her from shoulder to breast, blood roaring in his ears, his loins, as its heavy heat and resilience overflowed in his hand. She thrust her breast into his hold, inviting a harder kneading. He pinched her nipple, bent for a compulsive suckle as he came over her, groaning as her firmness cushioned his hardness.

"Elaahati al nareyah, you're beyond glorious."

Her face flushed with pleasure. "I've graduated from sorceress to goddess?"

"If there was more than goddess, you'd be that to me."

She dragged him down to her, drinking deep of his admiration and desire. Delight expanded through him as he melded their nakedness, fusing their mouths, his hands seeking all her secrets, taking every license, owning every inch. He brought her to orgasm around his fingers, before traveling down her body, draping her legs over his shoulders. She wantonly pressed her back to the mattress, arched her hips at him, opening herself wide for his devouring as he drank her overflowing pleasure.

When he finally slid up her body, she stopped him before he could join them. He rose from suckling her breasts, alarm hammering in his chest.

It dissipated at seeing her eyes, misty with emotion. "Will you stop punishing me and let me have you? Will you surrender to me?"

His own eyes stung with the poignancy of her need for his reciprocation, his need to cede all to her. *"Tulabatek awamer,* your demands are my commands, *ya naari."*

He turned on his back, taking her with him, letting her own every inch of him as he had her.

He threw back his head at the first touch of her lips on his erection. He'd never enjoyed this intimacy except with her. He'd never felt such a purity of desire as she delighted in pleasuring him. The look of blissful voracity that adorned her face as her lips wrapped around his girth, as she pumped and sucked him in abandon, murmuring and moaning her pleasure, soon had him stripped down to his savage male component. Blind with lust, with the need to dominate his female completely.

He still tried to pull away when she took him to the edge. She keened around his flesh, dug her fingers into his buttocks. He climaxed in scalding torrents, the pleasure agonizing as she greedily drank him.

Finally, reluctantly letting him slide out of her mouth, she pressed her flushed, moist face to his thigh. "We *are* even now. You've become an addiction, too."

"I won't concede this. I claim the deeper addiction, and more frequent need of your taste and pleasure as my fix."

She began to protest, but he dragged her beneath him, bore down on her, came between her eagerly splaying thighs and plunged into her flowing depths, the vise of heat and ecstasy she surrendered to him, captured him in. He knew the aggression of his passion sent her insane with lust, that the edge of pain from being barely able to accommodate him made her pleasure more explosive.

With every thrust, his every word detailing his pleasure at being inside her, she writhed beneath him, her hair rippling waves of titian gloss, her breathing fevered, her whole body straining around him.

Her answering confessions came thicker, became more fevered, deeper. "Haidar—I missed you…never felt alive without you, without this…your flesh in mine…do it all to me, give me all of you…"

He obeyed, strengthened his thrusts until she rippled around him and convulsions squeezed soft shrieks out of her, spasmed her inner flesh around his erection.

The force of her release smashed the last of his restraint. He roared, let go, his body all but exploding in ecstasy. He felt his essence flowing into her as he fed her pleasure to the last tremor, until her arms and legs fell off him in satiation.

Shuddering from the aftershocks of the most violent and

profound orgasm he'd ever attained, even with her, he collapsed on top of her, knowing she loved his weight anchoring her after the storm of pleasure had wreaked havoc on them. He felt her lips trembling on his forehead, heard his name in a litany of longing.

Tenderness swamped him. *"Ahebbek, ya naari, kamm ahebbek."*

She went still, her lips freezing on his face.

He rose on both arms, this unreasoning anxiety still so easy to trigger. It spiked to a heart-pummeling level. She was crying.

"That's the first time you've ever said you love me," she whispered.

Blood roared through his head in a riptide of regret. "I more than love you. *Ana aashagek,* I worship you and more, *ya hayat galbi.* And I'll never forgive myself for not telling you sooner."

She tugged him down for a searingly sweet kiss, letting him taste her tears of happiness. "If I forgive you, life of *my* heart, who are you not to? I hereby abolish all self-recriminations."

He could argue that she shouldn't. But her peace of mind depended on turning this page of their past. No one said he couldn't seek redemption in secret for, say, the rest of his life.

He wiped away her tears as he swept her on top of him. "As long as it's a two-way street."

She buried her face in his neck on a sob, nodded.

Soon, her breathing settled into the contented rhythm of deep sleep. He lay beneath her, still joined to her, feeling her blanket him in serenity and joy.

It was merciful that he *had* forgotten just how sublime making love to her was. Or maybe it was different now, with their maturity, their honesty about their emotions.

He encompassed her velvet firmness with caresses, letting awe and thankfulness and then sweet oblivion overtake him.

* * *

"What's *that?*"

From his kneeling position, Haidar grinned up at a stupefied Roxanne. "That is a piece from the Pride of Zohayd."

"What?" She snatched the jewelry box from his hands, gaped down at it. "It can't be. It's not possible to get a part of the treasure out of Zohayd without the national guard on its tail."

Now that she had taken the box, his stint at her feet was concluded. He rose, grinning in self-satisfaction. "You're talking to the Prince of Two Kingdoms here."

"You could be the Prince of Two *Planets* and those jewels wouldn't be allowed out of Zohayd for any reason. Certainly not to be my...*shabkah*..."

Gulping as if the word stuck in her throat, she ran trembling fingers over the piece he'd picked as her "tying" present, a sublimely worked, twenty-four-carat-gold web ring/bracelet encrusted with priceless diamonds and a one-of-a-kind emerald centerpiece.

Belief hit her like a bolt, had her stunned eyes jerking up to him. "God, it *is* the real thing, isn't it?"

He smiled at her, enjoying her flustered sequence of denial and realization to no end. "That *is* the whole point."

"B-but how is it possible that you have it?"

Something in her eyes wiped his smile away. "Are you thinking I...took it?" When she only continued to gape at him, bitterness seeped into him. "Or that as an accomplice to my mother's conspiracy, I got to keep some pieces...?"

She pounced on him, one hand covering his mouth. "Stop right there! I am *not* doubting you. I'm never gonna do that again, remember? I'm just...boggling."

He saw it. Her disbelief had nothing to do with him. Her belief in him *was* total.

Hurt evaporated like a dewdrop in a furnace, teasing taking over again. "Want to boggle some more? This is *the* piece."

Her mouth dropped open, remained like that for a whole minute.

Then she cried out, "No *way*. *The* first piece that Ezzat Aal Shalaan built the whole Pride of Zohayd treasure around? The piece that started the myth-turned-law of the Aal Shalaan's claim to the throne?"

"Nothing less would do what I feel for you justice."

She looked down at the magical beauty and intricacy of the piece. Suddenly she winced. "God, Haidar, no! It's too much of a responsibility. I would be scared to wear it. What if I damage it? What if I *lose* it? What if people realize it's the real deal?"

"The best way to ensure its and your safety is for you to remain no more than two inches away from me at all times."

She whacked the arm reaching for her. *"Haidar!"*

"Just kidding. If not by much." He picked up the hand that had inflicted such delicious pain, kissed its trembling palm. "You can say it's an uncanny imitation, never say it's *your* *shabkah*. Only we need know the truth and what it signifies as the centerpiece of a legend that has stood the test of time and inspired millions."

Her hand cupped his face, her smile trembling in incipient delight. "You think we have one in the making?"·

He took the ring/bracelet out of the box, fitted it on her left hand. "I know we do."

He claimed her in a long kiss until she surfaced with another exclamation. "But *how?* I mean getting *this*—" she raised her hand to gape at the masterpiece of craftsmanship again "—is up there with flying under your own power. And *when?* Your proposal wasn't premeditated. And after I blubbered out my acceptance, there wasn't enough time."

"You underestimate how fast I can get things done." At her warning look he raised his hands. "But your analytical powers are spot on, as usual. I arranged to get it as soon as I received your text informing me of our meeting here. That's why I was so late."

"It wasn't to make me wait an hour for each year I cost us apart?"

He smirked. "That did cross my mind, too."

"But you were waiting for the...*shabkah*..." She fluttered as she examined it again.

He pinched her delightful bottom. "I *could* have arrived at your specified time and had it delivered here."

"So you *were* messing with me." She pushed herself harder into his hand, giving him a better grip. "As you had a right to."

"A right I wouldn't have exercised if I thought I had it. I wanted to run here the second I got your message. But I also wanted to get my hands on your *shabkah,* to be the only one to touch it after Amjad."

"*King* Amjad? *He* brought it to you? As in, *himself?*"

Surprising her was such a joy. He had to keep doing it. "Who else would have such access to the Pride of Zohayd? And who else is mad enough to give me its cornerstone piece, for any reason?"

She nodded. "Yeah. It's said he has evolved from Mad Prince to Crazy King status." A tide of peach spread up her face as she rushed to add, "Which in my opinion is great. His methods are shocking, but their results are amazing. I think he's the most effective king in the region's history since King Kamal Aal Masood of Judar."

He chuckled, soothing her embarrassment. "Never worry about offending my sibling sensibilities. My oldest brother always had a method to his madness, but now it also has a name—Maram. His better ninety-nine percent, as he says."

"So you told him you wanted the Pride of Zohayd's origin piece, and he just gave it to you? How will he justify this—and this *will* come out—to his council, to the people of Zohayd?"

"He's going to tell them to *shut up* or he'll auction off the rest, as he threatened to do before he took the throne from Father."

"Wow." Her head shake was dazed, her lips twitching. "I bet I could fill volumes analyzing him and his methods."

"Just think—when you marry me, you'll have open access to that one-of-a-kind specimen as his sister-in-law."

She scrunched her face. "Yeah, that's the main reason I'm marrying you—so I can get my analytical paws on your big brother."

"How about getting those paws, analytical and every other kind, on me?"

She ran her *shabkah*-clad hand down his chest, gently scraping his flesh. "The problem will be in getting them *off* you."

He took her lips, pressed her hand harder, every abrasion a sledgehammer of arousal. "I only need them off to get work and self-maintenance out of the way. Then they're back on. And on."

She shuddered as he deepened their mouth-mating.

It didn't feel strictly like pleasure. "What is it, *ya naar rohi?*"

"*This*—" her gesture was eloquent with what raged between them "—fire of *my* soul." Her eyes were almost uncertain. "Are humans supposed to attain this kind of happiness?"

He crushed her to him, pledged, "I only know we are."

Eleven

"We are confident you are well ahead of your competitors.

Haidar swept his gaze from the man who'd just spouted such an unsubstantiated claim to his other supporters, who were regarding him as if he were hiding their Christmas presents.

For the past two weeks since he'd proposed to Roxanne they had left him no waking hour without intrusion, offering strategies, asking about his own, pushing for confirmation that he would go all out to claim the throne. Not to mention constantly pandering to his ego.

He sighed. "Let's not indulge in make-believe, please. Rashid is a formidable contender, an all-Azmaharian war hero—"

The group's spokesman cut in. "He's a fledgling in the world of finance and politics compared to you."

"A fledgling who flew out of the nest a fully grown vulture of the first order, and who might tear me apart if I turn my back on him like…I don't know, like I'm doing now while I pursue this quest? And then there is Jalal, who is the more—"

The man interrupted again. "Jalal is too Zohaydan. Yo

are the perfect combination we need, if you'll only take this more seriously."

"Like Rashid, you mean?" He huffed. "But aren't you claiming this is all about what's best for Azmahar? If he proves the better—"

"He isn't," another man insisted. "And neither is Jalal. But Rashid is forming alliances beyond his supporters. And Jalal has the kingdom's top politico-economic expert as his consultant."

Everything hit Pause inside Haidar.

There was only one person that could describe. Roxanne.

It was impossible. "You are misinformed about Jalal. Which makes me wonder about all the information you've been feeding me."

"We have proof," a third man said. "Photos of Jalal with Roxanne Gleeson for the past month, phone recordings—"

His heat shot up. "You're monitoring her phone?"

The man shook his head. "His. This is a major fight, and we will do anything to stop our adversary from gaining unfair advantage. And with her on his side, he certainly has that over you and Rashid. Not that we regret breaching her privacy. It's almost unethical to be supplying him with information she has come by from her job here."

Haidar didn't know what he said, or how the meeting came to an end. He found himself alone, paralyzed, in body and mind.

Then in the numb silence inside him, a voice rose. Serene, cajoling, knowing, explaining it all.

Roxanne was playing both of them. Until one became king. Then she'd pick him up like a ripe plum. She thought secrecy would even serve her if Rashid took the throne. She'd remain on his good side, maximize on his good opinion to win an even bigger role. While it would keep her options open with him and Jalal until she decided who would provide the most benefit to her. Probably Jalal. Putting up with a friend-turned-husband was one thing. Dealing with someone as emotionally and physically demanding as *him* was another. She might even dump them both and go for Rashid. And she'd get him. Not only was she irresistible in her own right, she had the insider info she needed to pull Rashid's strings.

He pressed both palms to his ears, shutting out that maddening, *mutilating* voice. The voice he now recognized.

His mother's.

That *was* her talking. She'd passed down to him the seeds of paranoia and mistrust and then fostered them every way she could. Listening to that voice had served him well in the cutthroat world of business. It had decimated his personal life.

He was done listening to her. He was done doubting Roxanne.

He would ask her about Jalal. And whatever she told him, it would be the truth.

End of story.

Haidar dived beneath the turquoise waters, surfaced with Roxanne wrapped around him. He squeezed her satiny flesh, ravaged her lips with smiling kisses that she reciprocated with enough ardor to turn the sea to steam. Though he'd just finished making love to her on the island, that hadn't even begun to satisfy him.

He slid his lips to her ear, gently bit her earlobe. "Race me back to the pier?"

She giggled, nipped his chin. "I have not turned into a dolphin yet. You'd have the fish cooked by the time I catch up."

"But you are a *saherah*. You can just use your magic."

Her eyes blasted him with unadulterated appreciation. "'Look who's talking' seems to comprise most of what I say to you these days."

She did make him feel as if he possessed magic. She made

him feel craved, treasured to his last cell. Just as he craved and treasured her.

He swept her into his arms, swam on his back with leisurely strokes in the still waters that had mercifully been untainted by the oil spill. She nestled into him, the largest part of his soul. His gaze swept what she called their oasis in the declining sun, luxuriated in feeling her through the silk medium of perfect-temperature water, in being with her in such a huge personal space. He had scheduled the estate caretakers to come only when she was at work.

Being here with her had long surpassed any heaven he'd ever heard about.

It would stay their secret heaven until the whole throne business was concluded. He didn't want to beat his opponents through the mass appeal of a fairy-tale wedding and the promise of the best queen the kingdom could hope for. He wanted to either take the throne by personal merit, or not at all. He also wanted to separate *them* from any tinge of business and politics.

They swam to the pier in languid silence, tapping into and feeding each other's energies and emotions in a closed circuit of harmony. Time stretched when they were together. The month since they'd found each other again felt like a year. More. He barely remembered his life before this month.

He certainly didn't want to remember the time after he'd lost her, when the knife kept twisting harder each time his siblings found their soul mates. Aliyah had found Kamal, Shaheen had Johara, Harres had Talia, and most shocking and improbable of all, Amjad had Maram. But he'd found Roxanne again, and at last had her for real, and this time forever. It was nothing short of a miracle.

He sighed, felt enveloped in the contentment and certainty only her embrace imbued him with.

Suddenly she wriggled, broke his hold, kicked away.

She laughed as he gave pursuit. Despite her earlier joke, she was such a strong swimmer, he almost didn't need to slow down for her to beat him to the pier. She pulled herself onto it in one agile move, stood in her flame-colored torture device of a swimsuit grinning down at him.

He took his time following her, to look his fill as she dried herself in brisk movements. Those grew languid as he neared, gathered her, cherished her every inch in caresses and kisses as she stroked him dry.

He lifted her in his arms and she clung around his neck as he walked to the house. "I was thinking of the incredible relationships my siblings have, and it made me think of Maram. I can't wait for you to meet her. You'll hit it off right out of the region."

She nuzzled his neck. "You never told me about her before."

He was realizing more and more how he'd shortchanged her. He never would again. "I adored her growing up. Still do. She's one of those rarities in life, an anomaly who liked me more than Jalal. Turned out my mother was behind throwing us together as part of her long-term plan to put me on the throne of Ossaylan, too. But all it did was create a special bond between us. And boy, did we milk *that* to give Amjad a well-deserved hard time."

"I'm not supposed to be jealous, right?"

"*Never* be, of anything in this world. *B'Ellahi*, I am yours."

His reward for the fervent vow was a kiss that almost had him taking her right there and to hell with showering and eating.

He pulled back, knowing she needed both. "As for Maram, she was my cherished friend, like Jalal was yours. I lost almost all touch with her as she went through the ordeals of her two marriages and temporary defection to the U.S., but once we saw each other again, it was like we never stopped being friends. I hope you can have the happiness of Jalal's friend-ship back, like I do Maram's."

He waited for her to tell him she *had* been seeing Jalal since he'd come back to Azmahar, that they had resumed their friendship.

She only looked away. "I would love that, too."

Arjooki, ya habibati...please, my love, trust me, tell me.

She didn't.

"You did *what*?"

Cherie's exclamation felt like nails against Roxanne's nerves.

She was again almost sorry she'd run to her friend with this.

But she hadn't been able to share it with her mother. Her mother, who was deliriously happy for the first time in...ever, after she'd told her about Haidar's proposal.

She'd told Cherie and Jalal, too, asked them to keep it a se-cret until the kingship issue was settled. Her mother had de-cided to cancel her retirement and come help her settle things faster so that the wedding could happen that much sooner.

Before any of that happened, she had to settle *this* mess.

She'd lied to Haidar point-blank, pretended she hadn't seen or heard from Jalal since the original breakup.

"You call this desert god of yours and tell him the truth right now, Roxanne. The more time you let pass between your...omission to tell him you've been seeing his twin be-hind his back, and helping him against him... God! What were you *thinking*?"

"It didn't happen that way!" she groaned. "I started this when Haidar was my worst enemy and Jalal my best friend. Suddenly Haidar is my fiancé and I'm helping Jalal, who's now his rival. I'm bound to Jalal by friendship and my word of honor, and to Haidar by love and everything else. But I couldn't tell him when he gave me the opening. It isn't my secret to tell."

"Famous last words." Cherie groaned, too. "You gotta fix this, and fast. Things like this can spiral and spoil everything. And your reconciliation with Haidar is too new and emotions too high."

"But Jalal still hasn't decided how to settle this whole mess between himself and Haidar!"

"Then tell Jalal to get his gorgeous butt settled, and tell your fiancé the truth before it messes up your newly fixed relationship!" Cherie came down beside her, hugged her to her side. "Listen, I took your advice and I'm getting back together with Ayman. We're even moving out of Azmahar so we can adopt. And as you jogged my mind back into the right place, I have to return the favor. Besides, the first time I nudged you to go after your man, you ended up with the biggest catch of the century in your net and the freaking origin piece of the Pride of Zohayd jewels on your hand. So am I good, or am I good?"

Roxanne hugged her. "You're superlative. I owe you far more than I can repay. And oh, I'm so happy about you and Ayman."

Cherie fluttered her lashes at her. "This means you forgive me for the mess I made of your immaculate place?"

A laugh burst out of her tight chest. "I've come to believe immaculate is overrated. And by the way, Haidar is asking if you've thought of his offer to finance your catering project."

"Have I *thought?*" Cherie jumped up in elation. "Apart from Ayman, I haven't thought of anything else. The moment you tell me you cleared things up with him, I'm hitting him with my proposal!"

After more nudges to tell Haidar, Cherie left Roxanne alone. In turmoil.

Cherie was right. It wasn't all about Jalal and her promise to keep his secret. She was scared to upset the perfection, the balance. Haidar would be disappointed she hadn't felt confident enough in their relationship to tell him. And after they'd agreed they'd never hide anything from each other again.

But she hadn't been hiding a thing. She just forgot about everything when she was with him. The only time she'd remembered Jalal lately had been when she'd told him, as her friend, about her and Haidar. The conflict of interest hadn't crossed her mind since Haidar's proposal. The only time she'd thought of the kingship issue in the past two weeks had been *with* Haidar, discussing his prospects and plans.

But Cherie was right again about needing to tell Haidar the truth. And Jalal was wrong about Haidar. Beneath the bitterness and alienation, Haidar loved him, or he wouldn't have been so hurt by his accusations. She should be the one to bring them back together, as she'd had an unwitting role in the formation of the fissure that had torn them apart. She'd summon her inner negotiator, go after Jalal—

The bell chime had her jumping.

God, her nerves *were* shot.

Which wasn't strange, with so much at stake.

She rushed to the door, opened it, found Jalal standing there.

"Gebna sert'el ott! Speak of the cat!" she exclaimed, dragged him in and into a hug.

Jalal chuckled, hugged her back. "And he comes bounding. *Konti b'tenteffi farweti ma'a meen*—who were you plucking my fur with?"

"I wasn't talking about you, just thinking of you, really."

"I should hope so, since you texted me to come over."

"But I…"

A key turned in the door. Cherie? She'd come back this soon?

Next second her skin almost pooled to the ground. *Haidar.*

Her heart stopped as she watched him walk in. One thing

became clear at once. He wasn't surprised to see Jalal. Which meant…

He was the one who'd arranged this. He must have texted Jalal from her phone when she'd been at his house a few hours ago.

He kept his eyes trained on Jalal. Her dazed gaze moved to Jalal, saw her same shock mixed with as powerful dismay, even if it had a different origin.

Silently, Haidar approached them as they stood frozen. He stopped feet away, bent slightly. A sharp smack jolted through her, had her heart stumbling like a horse on ice as her eyes searched out the sound's origin. A dossier on her coffee table.

Haidar straightened, still looking at Jalal. "These are the analysis reports that Roxanne supplied you with, that you were building your campaign around. I thought it only fair to inform you that they no longer constitute an edge, since I have them, too, in case they were the resource you were banking on to get ahead in this race."

Heartbeats blipped inside her chest, none pumping blood.

She didn't have to examine the dossier to know. It contained what he'd said. He knew. About her arrangement with Jalal.

But…he didn't seem angry. Or disappointed. He seemed… nothing. She could feel nothing from him. That opaque wall was up again. Was he hiding his disappointment or…or was this nothingness real?

And if it was…why? And how had he found out? When?

He'd brought up Jalal only yesterday, seemingly in passing, as if he knew nothing. But he couldn't have uncovered all that information during that time. So had he already known when he'd mentioned him? Had he been out to see if she'd come clean, or…?

A suspicion too terrible to contemplate detonated inside her.

No. She wasn't suspecting him again. She'd promised. Vowed.

But…*God*. He no longer seemed like the man she loved more than life. He was again the unknowable quantity, the inaccessible entity he'd been. The ice in his eyes was obliterating everything, leaving only stone-cold doubts and possibilities.

Could he have known about Jalal from the start? Investigated and put two and two together? He did have an uncanny deductive mind. It wasn't only possible. It was probable.

It appeared to be the truth.

But if he'd known, why had he never broached the subject?

Because you wouldn't have told him anything. Not as things stood between you at first.

So was that why he'd pursued her again? To get her to the point where she would talk? And supply him with better information than she'd given Jalal?

She *had* given him far more info than she had Jalal, thinking she'd been discussing Azmahar's future with her fiancé, discussing his major worries and plans.

Had it all been to beat Jalal at the game, again?

His mother's cold venom came back to her in a scalding rush of memory. Her pride in his long-term manipulative powers, which he'd inherited from her, the woman who'd plotted a region-smashing coup for over thirty years and almost pulled it off.

He'd once said he was her updated and improved version.

Would beating his brother again, for a throne no less, explain everything that had happened between them? Cold logic said that made more sense than what he'd professed. That his emotions had always been so powerful they'd survived the years of humiliation and alienation, that he loved her now above everything, as she loved him.

She had been wondering if it was possible for anyone to have all that, to be so happy. Had she been right to wonder, because no one could? Because none of it had been real?

Her world teetered on the verge of collapse.

Then he looked at her, his eyes empty. And it did.

Haidar looked at Roxanne and knew. Hearts did break.

She'd wept in his arms with pleasure, pledged love and allegiance. And she'd again hidden something of major importance from him. She hadn't trusted him. She hadn't put him first.

She never would.

He now faced the truth at last. What he'd been trying to run from all his life. His mother had been right. No one would ever love him. He inspired nothing but deficient, distorted emotions in those he loved. The proof was his mother's love itself. That monstrously manipulative, obsessively possessive emotion.

But he'd also been right about himself. He hadn't and wouldn't change. He couldn't live with having less than all of her.

That left him with none.

He stood facing the two people who had almost full monopoly of his emotions, formed the major part of his being. They'd again found it right to exclude him, to alienate him, to shut him out. All he could do now was relinquish hope. Accept that no matter what, he'd be forever alone.

"*That's* why you went after Roxanne this time?"

The dreadful growl yanked him out of his numbness.

He blinked, found Jalal in his face, his expression demonic.

"And to think I was agonizing over how to mend the rift between us, over what I accused you of, thinking I was wrong the more I thought about it. I was only wrong in imagining the depth of your depravity. I don't know how I never saw you for the monster you really are all our lives, but you deserve to be alone for the rest of yours. And although I didn't really want to be king, I'll now do anything to take that throne, to stop you from taking it."

Haidar barely registered his twin's abuse, let alone understood it. He saw nothing but the betrayal on Roxanne's face, felt nothing but the agony blasting off her.

But…why would she be the one feeling betrayed, agonized?

Because she was? By what? His choosing to save himself pain by giving up and walking away as she'd once done?

Suddenly, the enormity of his mistake crashed on him.

He'd been *wrong*.

If she chose to exclude him, he shouldn't consider it mistrust, or a deficiency of love. She had a right to help Jalal if she believed he'd make a better king. Even if she didn't, he was her friend, and she had every right to help him, do anything she chose to, his opinion or consent, or even knowledge, not required. And it stood independent from her relationship with him. It didn't affect her love for him, that she maintained parts of herself he had no access to.

He shouldn't ask for all of her. He had no right to it.

He would be happy, *grateful,* with any parts of her she chose to give him.

He reached for her, but something irresistible stopped him. He struggled with it, and something with the force of a sledgehammer struck him. The explosion detonated from the point of impact upward, shooting behind his eyes, jolting his brain.

Roxanne's receding figure buzzed in and out on his retinas, like a movie reel catching, blipping, burning.

Fighting off the disorientation, he tried to run after her. He slammed into something immovable. This time he fought back, moved it, ran after her, caught up with her.

Her hands smacked at him when he reached for her, her voice choked with the tears that ran down her cheeks. "What more do you want? I don't have any more information."

His vision was still warped, and so was his balance. He stumbled a step back when she pushed at him. "Roxanne… I don't…"

"You *didn't* need to go to all that trouble. You will surpass your rivals without any special strategy, just by being who you are. You are the best king Azmahar could hope for. The kingdom needs someone with such convoluted cunning to get it out of the maze of problems it's mired in. Not that I care what happens here anymore. I'm leaving. This time I'm never coming back."

He must still be disoriented. He didn't understand a thing she was saying. She was supposed to be slapping his face for daring to go back on his vow of always telling her everything. He should have told her how he felt, talked it out with her. Where did the throne come into this? What information was she talking about?

He caught her back and suddenly another pair of hands were on him, those he finally realized were Jalal's.

"Get your hands off her, Haidar," Jalal hissed. "This time, you're keeping them off her."

"I can fight my own battles, Jalal," she snapped.

"What battles? What are you two talking about...?" Something warm and wet trickled down his face, distracting him.

He put a hand to it, squinted at what came off. Blood.

He gaped at Jalal. "You hit me!"

"And you have the gall to be surprised?"

Haidar switched his stunned gaze between Jalal and Roxanne. They were in her bedroom. And he suddenly understood. What they were accusing him...worse, what they'd *condemned* him of.

And he did what he'd been seething to do for the past few decades. He smashed both fists into Jalal's shoulders, all his strength and years of fury and frustration behind the blow.

Jalal slammed into the wall with a crack that rattled the whole room. Roxanne gasped, stumbled against another wall. Haidar barely noticed, his focus pinned on Jalal who was now gaping at him.

Of course he was shocked. This was the first time in their lives that Haidar had ever shown him physical violence.

Before Jalal could recover, Haidar faced them both, his teeth bared. "Again? You're doing this again? You're passing judgment on me without giving me a chance to defend myself?"

Jalal straightened, returning his glare. "Excuse us as your actions *and* words speak so loudly they drown our attempts to exonerate you."

"So I compile a dossier on your activities and findings since you came here," Haidar hissed. "To prove that I was bound to find out, to show my disappointment that you both excluded me again, and you assume I got it from Roxanne? Worse, that I was with her just to get it? And for what? To foil your bid for the throne?"

Jalal's glare wavered. Haidar heard something distressed squeezing from Roxanne's chest.

He included her in his bitterness. "*Zain,* let's have this out. Air all your grievances and suspicions and accusations, the substantiated and imagined, and get this over with."

Jalal gave a disgusted grunt. "You mean an encore of the lifetime I spent doing just that? When every attempt at closeness or confrontation got me evasions, brush-offs and obstinate refusals to communicate or share anything?"

Haidar countered, "You mean those endless times when you were your pain-in-the-ass, intrusive, invasive, insensitive self?"

Jalal shrugged. "If you choose to see it that way."

"I do choose."

Jalal's gaze wavered. "Bottom line is, you always left me no recourse but to come to my own conclusions."

"And of course they had to be the worst ones. And you know why? Because I'm the walking reminder of what you lived your life afraid of facing, the personification of all your fears. What I spent my life trying not to rub your nose in. But, dearest twin, here it is, dry. You're part demon, too."

Jalal's teeth ground together.

Haidar smirked at the obvious hit. "You may not look it, and you may have convinced everyone you're all Aal Shalaan stock, but you haven't convinced *yourself.* You're as paranoid and suspicious and possessive and unreasonable where it comes to your loved ones as I am. You are my *twin,* Jalal, whether you like it or not."

Jalal's wolf eyes suddenly flared again. "I may be everything you said, Haidar, but *I* didn't finance our mother's conspiracy."

The jagged pain that slashed across Haidar's face yanked Roxanne out of the well of agitation she'd been spiraling in.

She'd misjudged him. Again. Hurt him, again. She was out of excuses this time.

She stepped between the two forces of nature snarling at each other, clung to Haidar's arm, whispered a tremulous "I'm sorry."

He tore his gaze away from his duel with Jalal, looked down at her. "Why? You think none of the things you said to me are true? Would you still be sorry if I tell you what Jalal just accused me of is the truth?"

Suppressing tears with all she had, she shook her head. "It can't be. It isn't."

"Why this sudden and unwavering trust?"

"Because this is my natural state now," she insisted. "I was having a minor breakdown minutes ago."

One eyebrow rose, the rest of his face unyielding. "It didn't look minor to me. And don't be so quick to anoint me with your unconditional belief. I *did* finance my mother's conspiracy."

She shook her head again, her heart bruising against her ribs. "Then you didn't know what the money was for."

OLIVIA GATES 177

"Minutes ago you assumed I screwed you over to get my-self a throne. Why assume a couple of years ago I wasn't will-ing to screw my whole family and kingdom over for an even bigger one?"

"Because you're no traitor." Her declaration was unequiv-ocal.

"You just thought I was," he persisted.

And tears flowed. "That was your mother's long-acting, insidious poison and my own fear that this—" her gesture be-tween them was eloquent with what they had, shared "—is too perfect to be true. The emotions you inspire in me are so over-powering, I'm still having trouble dealing with them, believ-ing they are reciprocated. Mainly—I can't believe my luck."

He regarded her dispassionately, his face impassive. "I still did finance my mother's conspiracy."

He was pushing her. Seeing when her trust would waver, crack.

She wiped away her tears, gave him a serene nod. "And I'm sure you're sorry about it and won't do anything like that again."

And he smiled.

She gasped in the breath she'd been unable to draw, her hand trembling on the terrible bruise spreading across his jaw as she attempted to smile back. "I'm cured. This time, irrevocably."

He dug his fingers into her hair, drew her up for a brief but fierce kiss. She moaned as she tasted his blood, the injury she'd been responsible for.

Seeming to realize this, he withdrew. "No more mistrust?"

"Insecurity," she insisted.

His nod was slow, accepting. Then he smiled again, a teas-ing sparkle entering his eyes. "And I won't monopolize your emotions and allegiance. You can love other people. Even Jalal here. *If* you must."

"As touching as this is, mind if you don't evade me again?"

Haidar turned to Jalal, that coolness that had once made both her and Jalal believe he was indifferent again coating his face. "You said you were agonizing about how to mend the rift between us, were no doubt loitering because you didn't know how to beg my forgiveness for your accusations."

Jalal took a threatening step closer. "Now, listen here—"

Haidar cut him off smoothly. "You wanted to because you thought they were wrong. What rationalization did you come up with for my actions to think that?"

Glowering at Haidar, Jalal exhaled. "I thought you didn't know why she wanted the money, but being the stupid sap that you are when it comes to her, you gave it to her without question."

Haidar's smile was the essence of concession and self-deprecation. "You think *she's* that stupid? She asked me for money over many years, every time with a reason, saying she couldn't ask our father, and didn't have enough money herself. I realized both were lies, assumed she demanded it as…tribute from me, as a proof of love and loyalty. Once I understood this, I sometimes gifted her with major sums, just because. I never suspected she had an insurrectionist agenda. The worst I suspected was that she'd do nothing philanthropic with it."

Jalal exhaled. "And you still gave it to her."

Haidar echoed his resignation. "It might seem unacceptable to you, and you must think it unbelievable I'd have this inexplicable soft *and* blind spot, but I do love her. I don't think I can stop."

Jalal drove his hands into his hair, wiped them down his face. "I can't stop, either. After all she's done, all she's cost us, I was right there with you, pleading for exile instead of imprisonment. *B'Ellahi,* I even call her regularly and drop by when I can."

***

That was a surprise to Haidar. "She didn't tell me. Still plotting, I see."

But then he *was* resigned that she always would be, lived wondering what her next strike would be.

"So…aren't you going to ask me about the other parts of her plans that I seemed involved in? What made you assume I was party to them?" He rubbed his jaw, only now registering the pain. "*Ya Ullah,* how I wanted to break *your* jaw when you intimated that."

"I thought she gave you what must have seemed like unrelated tasks that you couldn't have realized were cogs in the machine of her plan. Except after the fact." Contrition finally appeared in Jalal's eyes. "But I wanted *you* to tell me that."

"I didn't want to tell you anything. I wanted to smash your face in." Haidar smiled as all the remembered pain seeped away. "And you need to get to know me from scratch, like Roxanne needed to, if you don't realize why I didn't share details of my involvement with you or with anyone else. I had suspicion trained on me by the sheer evidence of my existence, by being the one she'd orchestrated all this for. I wasn't about to add my own sonly indiscretions to make a better case against myself. When you discovered them, like the relentless wolf that you are, and faced me, I was so…angry at myself, at you, I refused to defend myself. If you didn't know me enough to know your accusations were ludicrous, I decided *I* didn't want to know *you* at all. Of course I regretted it the moment I walked away. And of course I didn't know how to walk back into your life. I thought you would come to me, as you always did. You didn't."

"I wanted to," Jalal groaned. "Every single second of the past two years. I didn't know how to, either…"

Suddenly Jalal dragged Haidar into a rough hug.

* * *

Roxanne's tears flowed as Haidar stiffened, then groaned and sagged in his twin's hold. Then he hugged him back.

The poignancy of the moment drowned her, her heart battering her insides in delight as she felt the two men who mattered most to her begin to re-form their damaged bond. The man she was born to love, and the brother she'd longed to have, becoming what they should have always been, each other's sanctuary, and hers.

She watched them for as long as she could bear. Then she pounced on them, hugged them both with all her strength, pouring the tears of her relief, love and thankfulness on both their chests.

They at once took her in, at last acknowledging and delighting in the other's love, for one another, and for her.

It was Jalal who pulled back first, smirking at Haidar. "This doesn't mean I'm letting you become king."

Haidar's fist landed in a playful shove against his chin. "And this doesn't mean I don't owe you a broken jaw."

Jalal's gaze narrowed on him ponderously. "You *have* changed. You would have never joked about using your fists."

"I have changed." Haidar hugged her off the ground, gazing at her adoringly. "You're looking at the fuel of my metamorphosis."

Jalal cleared his throat, a bedeviling, knowing look directed at both of them. "*And* this is my cue to leave you two doves to coo to each other and go see if Rashid has already taken over while we indulged in our biannual twinly showdown."

Haidar gave him a considering look. "Maybe we should let him."

Jalal only gaped at him.

Then he directed a stern look at Roxanne. "Whatever softener you're using on him, ease up."

Giving them both a grinning salute, he walked out.

Roxanne hugged Haidar harder, buried smiles and tears into his expansive chest. "Forgive me."

A tender finger below her chin raised her face to his. "As long as you do me." She burst out laughing. He threw his head back and joined her. "That, too. Regularly."

She nestled deeper into his embrace. "And always. Along with everything else."

He squeezed her tight, a tremor passing through his great body at yet another, and this time last, averted heartache. "I'm holding you to that."

She nodded against his heart. "For as long as we both shall live. And beyond."

Epilogue

"Azmahar is and will always be a major part of who I am, and its people are my people. I will always be at its service, will do anything to mend the damage my closest kin have done to it."

Applause spread like thunder in the Qobba ballroom.

Roxanne's heart expanded until she felt it would burst with pride. Haidar had asked her to arrange this event with all the representatives of Azmahar's tribal councils. After his opening words, there was no doubt. They loved him. Believed in him.

The ruler of her heart and life was born to be king.

He was going on. "I am here today to make two announcements. The first is that I have asked for *Al Sayedah* Roxanne Gleeson's hand in marriage, and she has honored me by accepting. Our wedding will be held at her earliest convenience and readiness."

Roxanne's jaw dropped. B-but they'd agreed not...

"And with the pledge of my service and support to Azmahar unchangeable for as long as I live, I make the second announcement. I am withdrawing my candidacy for the throne."

Before anyone could react, before her heart found its next

beat, he was stepping down from the podium, walking toward her.

The moment he reached her, she smacked him.

Murmurs interspersed with laughter buzzed through the ballroom.

"I had to out us." He caught her hand, pressed it to his lips, then to his heart. "I couldn't take having no one cleaning the kitchen after our Cherie-inspired culinary adventures any longer."

She smacked him with her other hand. "Don't even try to joke! When did you reach that monumental decision, and how dare you spring it on me like this?"

"I knew we'd have this argument, and I wanted to have it only once. My mind is made up, *ya naar galbi,* fire of my heart."

"Without telling me?" she seethed. "What about your vow that you'd tell me everything."

"It's right here, where it will always be. But this is not about me. This is for Azmahar's best."

"It's for Azmahar to choose its best, and if it chooses you, you're damn well becoming king whether you like it or not!"

"And do you, without emotions and hormones, think I'm as qualified as Jalal or Rashid for the job, now of all times?"

"Qualified and more, for any throne in the world."

"That's *habibati* talking." His smile was all indulgence as he led her out of the ballroom.

"No, it isn't," she persisted, temperature rising another notch. "Personally, you're everything a king should be, and more."

"But there's more to me than what I am personally. You of all people know how my background—read, my mother—could mess things up. I don't believe I'm the one who can induce the best climate in the kingdom. Not in the top chair. I can do a lot of good from the sidelines, though. As I intend to, with you by my side as my princess. And consultant. I already told Jalal he shouldn't expect your exclusive services in that area."

She opened her mouth to protest and he closed it for her with a kiss. "I thought I would redeem myself by taking the throne and fixing what my mother and her family had destroyed. But I realized I was playing into her hands. The hands I can feel all over my candidacy. She wants me to become king, would do anything to achieve her objective. I believe she's still doing it. Stepping down is the only way to spoil her plans. To outrun her shadow. That will be my true redemption."

After collecting her jaw off the floor, Roxanne rasped, "I don't believe I'm saying this, but I'm on her side on this one. *That* throne you do deserve, and would be perfect for."

Haidar's smile was unperturbed, his determination unwavering. "And you think she'd stop after I'm king? From experience, she'd have more in store, and not anything for the general good. She's my mother, and I'll always be her son, will always serve her and take care of her, but I'm not giving her the chance to use me, or steer my life, *our* lives, anymore. It's as simple as that."

She stopped, realized they were in that corridor at the very spot where he'd once driven her to ecstasy, clung to him. "Haidar, it's not—"

"Can you possibly be that simple?"

Roxanne lurched at hearing the dark drawl, at feeling the presence that made all her hairs stand on end. She felt Haidar stiffen before he turned away. To face Rashid.

Haidar cocked his head at him, his lips twitching. "I'm beginning to think you have a teleportation device, Rashid. Though your materialization is welcome this time. If only to serve as a cue to move on to better topics." He looked back at her, eyes filling with intimacy and indulgence. "Like talking wedding and honeymoon plans."

Roxanne's heart fluttered. With delight at what Haidar was saying, agitation at what he'd just done and anxiety at Rashid's approach.

Rashid stopped a couple of steps away, drawing both her and Haidar's focus back to him.

His eyes bored into Haidar. "Don't tell me you think you can escape my payback by stepping down?"

Haidar shook his head, sighed.

Roxanne put herself between them. "Sheikh Aal Munsoori, I'm convinced there has been a tragic misunderstanding that's led to the current regrettable state of affairs between you and Haidar. But I am confident that we will be able to resolve the situation, and restore your relationship to its former closeness."

Rashid's darker-than-the-night eyes regarded her with nerve-rattling stillness, assessing, contemplating.

Then he gave her a smile that made goose bumps storm over her body. "I told Haidar you were very good. I was wrong. I'm now in possession of enough data to know you're superlative. But it's evident you're blinded by emotions—for now. So marry him, if you currently believe you can't live without him. But also do what will count, in your life and that of others. Join my team." Rashid suddenly picked up her hand, took it to his lips for a brief electrifying peck, his eyes glittering onyxes as he looked down at her. "Just name your terms."

Haidar growled something exasperated at her back. "Don't even think of using Roxanne as part of your payback plans."

Rashid slanted his gaze back to him, one formidable eyebrow arching sardonically. "I think too much of her and too little of you to do that. This is a legitimate offer, and all for her. She will end up wising up and dumping you as she should all on her own."

"Don't hold your breath, or only if you can for the rest of our lives. This is how long Roxanne and me will last. As for you, I'm shoving peace down your throat whether you like it or not."

"And you'll do that while hiding behind your lady?"

Haidar stepped before her and in Rashid's face, his face relaxing in a smile. "Your inflammatory tactics won't get a rise from me again, Rashid. This war is over."

Rasid's summing-up gaze lengthened until Roxanne felt she'd snap with the tension.

Then in ultimate calmness, he said, "I'll grant you only a ceasefire, Haidar, for Ms. Gleeson's sake. Once the honeymoon is over, the war resumes."

Then with a courteous bow to her, he walked away.

Roxanne let out the breath that had been clogged in her lungs on a tremulous exhalation. "We really need to find out what he believes he has against you. Fast."

Haidar exhaled heavily. *"Aih."* He suddenly lifted her off the ground in a fierce hug, smiling full down at her. "After a very, *very* prolonged honeymoon."

Before she could think of a response, he pressed her against the wall, took her lips in a kiss that wiped away anything else but him from her mind.

She surfaced from his kiss struggling to remember the other paramount issue at hand, gasped, "But promise me another thing. If Azmahar demands you on the throne anyway, you won't refuse, for any reason."

"I promise." His solemn expression turned bedeviling as he winked at her. "If I can prove the whole population wasn't mass-manipulated by my mother, that is."

"Haidar!"

He kissed her indignation away, had her objections and arguments blurring before he withdrew to look down at her, grinning teasingly. "So what do you think it is about me that makes the women in my life want to put me on a throne?"

She sighed, dreamily, resignedly. "You'd be gorgeous on one?"

His eyes twinkled. "I thought I was gorgeous on, in and out of anything."

She surrendered, dragged him down for another life-affirming kiss. "You are that, and then awesome."

A long time later, after loving her into the night, he hugged her more securely into his body, whispered against her cooling cheek, "I do promise, *ya naar hayati*. I will answer the call of duty if Azmahar issues it and I'm certain it has made the right decision. But know this. For myself, I crave only your love, aspire only to having you for my lover, my princess, my partner in everything. I want us to work together to bring Azmahar back to its former glory. Whether I become king or not."

She turned to look into his eyes, saw his heart, let him see hers and pledged, "I promise you that, too. And everything else that you yet have to wish for or imagine…"

* * * * *

Get swept away
with the next DESERT KNIGHTS *book*
THE SHEIKH'S CLAIM,
Jalal's explosively passionate story!
September 2012
Only from Olivia Gates and Harlequin Desire!

COMING NEXT MONTH from Harlequin Desire®
AVAILABLE JULY 2, 2012

#2167 A SCANDAL SO SWEET
Ann Major

When a billionaire entrepreneur and an actress with a scandalous past are reunited, they quickly find that the fire of their passion has never died.

#2168 GILDED SECRETS
The Highest Bidder
Maureen Child

Can he seduce the single mother's secrets out of her before they bring the world's most glamorous auction house to its knees?

#2169 STRICTLY TEMPORARY
Billionaires and Babies
Robyn Grady

Stranded in a snowstorm with an abandoned baby, two strangers create their own heat in each other's arms.

#2170 THE CINDERELLA ACT
The Drummond Vow
Jennifer Lewis

A hedge-fund billionaire falls for his housekeeper, but will duty to his pregnant ex-wife and class differences keep them from finding true love?

#2171 A MAN OF PRIVILEGE
Sarah M. Anderson

When a blue-blooded lawyer falls for his impoverished witness, it's a conflict of interest and a clash of different worlds.

#2172 MORE THAN HE EXPECTED
Andrea Laurence

A no-strings fling? That's what this avowed bachelor thought he wanted...until he finds his past lover pregnant—and sexier than ever!

REQUEST YOUR FREE BOOKS!

2 FREE NOVELS PLUS 2 FREE GIFTS!

ALWAYS POWERFUL, PASSIONATE AND PROVOCATIVE

YES! Please send me 2 FREE Harlequin Desire® novels and my 2 FREE gifts (gifts are worth about $10). After receiving them, if I don't wish to receive any more books, I can return the shipping statement marked "cancel." If I don't cancel, I will receive 6 brand-new novels every month and be billed just $4.30 per book in the U.S. or $4.99 per book in Canada. That's a saving of at least 14% off the cover price! It's quite a bargain! Shipping and handling is just 50¢ per book in the U.S. and 75¢ per book in Canada.* I understand that accepting the 2 free books and gifts places me under no obligation to buy anything. I can always return a shipment and cancel at any time. Even if I never buy another book, the two free books and gifts are mine to keep forever.

225/326 HDN FEF3

Name _____ (PLEASE PRINT)

Address _____ Apt. #

City _____ State/Prov. _____ Zip/Postal Code

Signature (if under 18, a parent or guardian must sign)

Mail to the **Reader Service:**

IN U.S.A.: P.O. Box 1867, Buffalo, NY 14240-1867
IN CANADA: P.O. Box 609, Fort Erie, Ontario L2A 5X3

Not valid for current subscribers to Harlequin Desire books.

Want to try two free books from another line?
Call 1-800-873-8635 or visit www.ReaderService.com.

* Terms and prices subject to change without notice. Prices do not include applicable taxes. Sales tax applicable in N.Y. Canadian residents will be charged applicable taxes. Offer not valid in Quebec. This offer is limited to one order per household. All orders subject to credit approval. Credit or debit balances in a customer's account(s) may be offset by any other outstanding balance owed by or to the customer. Please allow 4 to 6 weeks for delivery. Offer available while quantities last.

Your Privacy—The Reader Service is committed to protecting your privacy. Our Privacy Policy is available online at www.ReaderService.com or upon request from the Reader Service.

We make a portion of our mailing list available to reputable third parties that offer products we believe may interest you. If you prefer that we not exchange your name with third parties, or if you wish to clarify or modify your communication preferences, please visit us at www.ReaderService.com/consumerschoice or write to us at Reader Service Preference Service, P.O. Box 9062, Buffalo, NY 14269. Include your complete name and address.

HDES11B

New York Times *and* USA TODAY *bestselling author Vicki Lewis Thompson returns with yet another irresistible cowpoke! Meet Mathew Tredway—cowboy, horse whisperer and honorary Son of Chance.*

Read on for a sneak peek from the bestselling miniseries SONS OF CHANCE:

LEAD ME HOME
Available July 2012 only from Harlequin® Blaze™.

As MATTHEW RETURNED to the corral and Houdini, the taste of Aurelia's mouth was on his lips and her scent clung to his clothes. He'd briefly satisfied the craving growing within him, and like a light snack before a meal, it would have to do.

When he'd first walked into the kitchen, his mind had been occupied with the challenge of training Houdini. He'd thought his concentration would hold long enough to get some carrots, ask about the corn bread and leave before succumbing to Aurelia's appeal. He'd miscalculated. Within a very short time, desire had claimed every brain cell.

Although seducing her this morning was out of the question, his libido had demanded some sort of satisfaction. He'd tried to deny that urge and had nearly made it out of the house. Apparently his willpower was no match for the temptation of Aurelia's mouth, though, and he'd turned around.

If he'd ever felt this kind of desperate need for a woman, he couldn't recall it. During the night, as he'd lain in his narrow bunk listening to the cowhands snore, he'd searched for an explanation as to why Aurelia affected him this way.

Sometime in the early-morning hours he'd come up with

HBEXP0712

the answer. After years of dating women who were rolling stones like he was, he'd developed an itch for a hearth-and-home kind of woman. Aurelia, with her cooking skills and voluptuous body, could give him that.

With luck, once he'd scratched this particular itch, he'd be fine again. He certainly hoped so, because he had no intention of giving up his career, and travel was a built-in requirement. Plus he liked to travel and had no real desire to stay in one spot and become domesticated.

Tonight he'd say all that to Aurelia, because he didn't want her going into this with any illusions about permanence. He figured that when the right guy came along, she'd get married and have kids.

Too bad that guy wouldn't be him....

Will Aurelia be the one to corral this cowboy for good?
Find out in: LEAD ME HOME

Available July 2012
wherever Harlequin® Blaze™ books are sold.

This summer, celebrate everything Western
with Harlequin® Books!

www.Harlequin.com/Western

HBEXP0712